PRAISE FOR JOHN GRISHAM'S
Bleachers

"*Bleachers* is touching not just because of its all-American story, but because its author is so sincere in telling it that it hurts."
—*The Boston Globe*

"Engaging... There are echoes of Jason Miller's Pulitzer Prize–winning play, *That Championship Season*, and Irwin Shaw's classic short story, *The Eight-Yard Run*."
—*USA Today*

"This is a book designed to make a certain type of grown man cry, and the author knows exactly which buttons to push: dying father-figures, the scars of tough love, middle-aged regret and the mythology of the gridiron."
—*The New York Times Book Review*

"Grisham's theme is comfortably romantic: You can go home again... a reminder of what an effortless storyteller Grisham can be."
—*The Columbus Dispatch*

ALSO BY JOHN GRISHAM

A DELL BOOK

NEW YORK   LONDON   TORONTO   SYDNEY   AUCKLAND

Bleachers

John Grisham

BLEACHERS
A Dell Book

PUBLISHING HISTORY
Doubleday hardcover edition published October 2003
Dell mass market edition / July 2004

Published by
Bantam Dell
A Division of Random House, Inc.
New York, New York

This is a work of fiction. Names, characters, places, and incidents either
are the product of the author's imagination or are used fictitiously. Any
resemblance to actual persons, living or dead, events, or locales is entirely
coincidental.

Library of Congress Catalog Card Number: 2003055534

ISBN 0-440-24200-2

Manufactured in the United States of America
Published simultaneously in Canada

OPM 10 9 8 7 6 5 4 3 2 1

Bleachers

Tuesday

The road to Rake Field ran beside the school, past the old band hall and the tennis courts, through a tunnel of two perfect rows of red and yellow maples planted and paid for by the boosters, then over a small hill to a lower area covered with enough asphalt for a thousand cars. The road stopped in front of an immense gate of brick and wrought iron that announced the presence of Rake Field, and beyond the gate was a chain-link fence that encircled the hallowed ground. On

Friday nights, the entire town of Messina waited for the gate to open, then rushed to the bleachers where seats were claimed and nervous pregame rituals were followed. The black, paved pasture around Rake Field would overflow long before the opening kickoff, sending the out-of-town traffic into the dirt roads and alleys and remote parking zones behind the school's cafeteria and its baseball field. Opposing fans had a rough time in Messina, but not nearly as rough as the opposing teams.

Driving slowly along the road to Rake Field was Neely Crenshaw, slowly because he had not been back in many years, slowly because when he saw the lights of the field the memories came roaring back, as he knew they would. He rolled through the red and yellow maples, bright in their autumn foliage. Their trunks had been a foot thick in Neely's glory days, and now their branches touched above him and their leaves dropped like snow and covered the road to Rake Field.

It was late in the afternoon, in October, and a soft wind from the north chilled the air.

He stopped his car near the gate and stared

at the field. All movements were slow now, all thoughts weighted heavily with sounds and images of another life. When he played the field had no name; none was needed. Every person in Messina knew it simply as The Field. "The boys are on The Field early this morning," they would say at the cafés downtown. "What time are we cleaning up The Field?" they would ask at the Rotary Club. "Rake says we need new visitors' bleachers at The Field," they would say at the boosters' meeting. "Rake's got 'em on The Field late tonight," they would say at the beer joints north of town.

No piece of ground in Messina was more revered than The Field. Not even the cemetery.

After Rake left they named it after him. Neely was gone by then, of course, long gone with no plans to return.

Why he was returning now wasn't completely clear, but deep in his soul he'd always known this day would come, the day somewhere out there in the future when he was called back. He'd always known that Rake would eventually die, and of course there would be a funeral with hundreds of former players packed around the casket, all wearing their Spartan green, all mourning the loss of a legend they loved and hated. But he'd told himself many times that he would never return to The Field as long as Rake was alive.

In the distance, behind the visitors' stands, were the two practice fields, one with lights. No other school in the state had such a luxury, but then no other town worshiped its football as thoroughly and collectively as Messina. Neely could hear a coach's whistle and the thump and grunts of bodies hitting each other as the latest Spartan team got ready for Friday night. He walked through the gate and across the track, painted dark green of course.

The end zone grass was manicured and suitable for putting, but there were a few wild sprigs inching up the goalpost. And there was a patch or two of weeds in one corner, and now that he'd noticed Neely looked even closer and saw untrimmed growth along the edge of the track. In the glory days dozens of volunteers gathered every Thursday afternoon and combed The Field with gardening shears, snipping out every wayward blade of grass.

The glory days were gone. They left with Rake. Now Messina football was played by mortals, and the town had lost its swagger.

Coach Rake had once cursed loudly at a well-dressed gentleman who committed the sin of stepping onto the sacred Bermuda grass of The Field. The gentleman backtracked quickly, then walked around the sideline, and when he drew closer Rake realized he had just cursed the Mayor of Messina. The Mayor was offended. Rake didn't care. No one walked on his field. The Mayor, unaccustomed to being cursed, set in motion an ill-fated effort to fire Rake, who shrugged it off. The locals defeated the Mayor four to one as soon as his name appeared on the next ballot.

In those days, Eddie Rake had more political clout in Messina than all the politicians combined, and he thought nothing of it.

Neely stuck to the sideline and slowly made his way toward the home stands, then he stopped cold and took a deep breath as the pregame jitters hit him hard. The roar of a long-ago crowd came back, a crowd packed tightly together up there, in the bleachers, with the band in the center of things blaring away with its endless renditions of the Spartan fight song. And on the sideline just a few feet away, he could see number 19 nervously warming up as the mob worshiped him. Number 19 was a high school all-American, a highly recruited quarterback with a golden arm, fast feet, plenty of size, maybe the greatest Messina ever produced.

Number 19 was Neely Crenshaw in another life.

He walked a few steps along the sideline, stopped at the fifty where Rake had coached hundreds of games, and looked again at the silent bleachers where ten thousand people once gathered on Friday nights to pour their emotions upon a high school football team.

The crowds were half that now, he'd heard.

Fifteen years had passed since number 19 had thrilled so many. Fifteen years since Neely had played on the sacred turf. How many times had he promised himself he would never do what he was now doing? How many times had he sworn he would never come back?

On a practice field in the distance a coach blew a whistle and someone was yelling, but Neely barely heard it. Instead he was hearing the drum corps of the band, and the raspy, unforgettable voice of Mr. Bo Michael on the public address, and the deafening sound of the bleachers rattling as the fans jumped up and down.

And he heard Rake bark and growl, though his coach seldom lost his cool in the heat of battle.

The cheerleaders were over there—bouncing, chanting, short skirts, tights, tanned and firm legs. Neely had his pick back then.

His parents sat on the forty, eight rows down from the press box. He waved at his mother before every kickoff. She spent most of the game in prayer, certain he would break his neck.

The college recruiters got passes to a row of chair-backed seats on the fifty, prime seating. Someone counted thirty-eight scouts for the Garnet Central game, all there to watch number 19. Over a hundred colleges wrote letters; his father still kept them. Thirty-one offered full scholarships. When Neely signed with Tech, there was a press conference and headlines.

Ten thousand seats up in the bleachers, for a town with a population of eight thousand. The math had never worked. But they piled in from the county, from out in the sticks where there was nothing else to do on Friday night. They got their paychecks and bought their beer, and they came to town, to The Field where they clustered in one raucous pack at the north end of the stands and made more noise than the students, the band, and the townsfolk combined.

When he was a boy, his father had kept him away from the north end. "Those county people" down there were drinking and sometimes fighting and they yelled foul language at the officials. A few years later, number 19 adored the racket made by those county people, and they certainly adored him.

The bleachers were silent now, waiting. He moved slowly down the sideline, hands stuck deep in his pockets, a forgotten hero whose star had faded so quickly. The Messina quarterback for three seasons. Over a hundred touchdowns. He'd never lost on this field. The games came back to him, though he tried to block them out. Those days were gone, he told himself for the hundredth time. Long gone.

In the south end zone the boosters had erected a giant scoreboard, and mounted around it on large white placards with bold green lettering was the history of Messina football. And thus the history of the town. Undefeated seasons in 1960 and 1961, when Rake was not yet thirty years old. Then in 1964 The Streak began, with perfect seasons for the rest of that decade and into the next. A month after Neely was born in 1970, Messina lost to South Wayne in the state championship, and The Streak was over. Eighty-four wins in a row, a national record at that time, and Eddie Rake was a legend at the age of thirty-nine.

Neely's father had told him of the unspeakable gloom that engulfed the town in the days after that loss. As if eighty-four straight victories were not enough. It was a miserable winter, but Messina endured. Next season, Rake's boys went 13–0 and slaughtered South Wayne for the state title. Other state championships followed, in '74, '75, and '79.

Then the drought. From 1980 until 1987, Neely's senior year, Messina went undefeated each season, easily won its conference and play-offs, only to lose in the state finals. There was discontent in Messina. The locals in the coffee shops were not happy. The old-timers longed for the days of The Streak. Some school in California won ninety in a row and the entire town of Messina was offended.

To the left of the scoreboard, on green placards with white lettering, were the tributes to the greatest of all Messina heroes. Seven numbers had been retired, with Neely's 19 being the last. Next to it was number 56, worn by Jesse Trapp, a linebacker who played briefly at Miami then went to prison. In 1974, Rake had retired number 81, worn by Roman Armstead, the only Messina Spartan to play in the NFL.

Beyond the south end zone was a field house that any small college would envy. It had a weight room and lockers and a visitors' dressing room with carpet and showers. It too was built by the boosters after an intense capital campaign that lasted one winter and consumed the entire town. No expense was spared, not for the Messina Spartans football team. Coach Rake wanted weights and lockers and coaches' offices, and the boosters practically forgot about Christmas.

There was something different now, something Neely had not seen before. Just past the gate that led to the field house there was a monument with a brick base and a bronze bust on it. Neely walked over to take a look. It was Rake, an oversized Rake with wrinkles on the forehead and the familiar scowl around the eyes, yet just a hint of a smile. He wore the same weathered Messina cap he'd worn for decades. A bronze Eddie Rake, at fifty, not the old man of seventy. Under it was a plaque with a glowing narrative, including the details that almost anyone on the streets of Messina could rattle off from memory—thirty-four years as Coach of the Spartans, 418 wins, 62 losses, 13 state titles, and from 1964 to 1970 an undefeated streak that ended at 84.

It was an altar, and Neely could see the Spartans bowing before it as they made their way onto the field each Friday night.

The wind picked up and scattered leaves in front of Neely. Practice was over and the soiled and sweaty players were trudging toward the field house. He didn't want to be seen, so he walked down the track and through a gate. He climbed up thirty rows and sat all alone in the bleachers, high above Rake Field with a view of the valley to the east. Church steeples rose above the gold and scarlet trees of Messina in the distance. The steeple on the far left belonged to the

Methodist church, and a block behind it, unseen from the bleachers, was a handsome two-story home the town had given to Eddie Rake on his fiftieth birthday.

And in that home Miss Lila and her three daughters and all the rest of the Rakes were now gathered, waiting for the Coach to take his last breath. No doubt the house was full of friends, too, with trays of food covering the tables and flowers stacked everywhere.

Were any former players there? Neely thought not.

———

The next car into the parking lot stopped near Neely's. This Spartan wore a coat and tie, and as he walked casually across the track, he, too, avoided stepping onto the playing surface. He spotted Neely and climbed the bleachers.

"How long you been here?" he asked as they shook hands.

"Not long," Neely said. "Is he dead?"

"No, not yet."

Paul Curry caught forty-seven of the sixty-three touchdown passes Neely threw in their three-year career together. Crenshaw to Curry, time and time again, practically unstoppable. They had been cocaptains. They were close friends who'd drifted apart over the years. They still called each other three or four times a year. Paul's grandfather built the first Messina bank, so his future had been sealed at birth. Then he married a local girl from another prominent family. Neely was the best man, and the wedding had been his last trip back to Messina.

"How's the family?" Neely asked.

"Fine. Mona's pregnant."

"Of course she's pregnant. Five or six?"

"Only four."

Neely shook his head. They were sitting three feet apart, both gazing into the distance, chatting but preoccupied. There was noise from the field house as cars and trucks began leaving.

"How's the team?" Neely asked.

"Not bad, won four lost two. The coach is a young guy from Missouri. I like him. Talent's thin."

"Missouri?"

"Yeah, nobody within a thousand miles would take the job."

Neely glanced at him and said, "You've put on some weight."

"I'm a banker and a Rotarian, but I can still outrun you." Paul stopped quickly, sorry that he'd blurted out the last phrase. Neely's left knee was twice the size of his right. "I'm sure you can," Neely said with a smile. No harm done.

They watched the last of the cars and trucks speed away, most of them squealing tires or at least trying to. A lesser Spartan tradition.

Then things were quiet again. "Do you ever come here when the place is empty?" Neely asked.

"I used to."

"And walk around the field and remember what it was like back then?"

"I did until I gave it up. Happens to all of us."

"This is the first time I've come back here since they retired my number."

"And you haven't given it up. You're still living back then, still dreaming, still the all-American quarterback."

"I wish I'd never seen a football."

"You had no choice in this town. Rake had

us in uniforms when we were in the sixth grade. Four teams—red, blue, gold, and black, remember? No green because every kid wanted to wear green. We played Tuesday nights and drew more fans than most high schools. We learned the same plays Rake was calling on Friday night. The same system. We dreamed of being Spartans and playing before ten thousand fanatics. By the ninth grade Rake himself was supervising our practices and we knew all forty plays in his book. Knew them in our sleep."

"I still know them," Neely said.

"So do I. Remember the time he made us run slot-waggle-right for two solid hours in practice?"

"Yeah, because you kept screwin' up."

"Then we ran bleachers until we puked."

"That was Rake," Neely mumbled.

"You count the years until you get a varsity jersey, then you're a hero, an idol, a cocky bastard because in this town you can do no wrong. You win and win and you're the king of your own little world, then poof, it's gone. You play your last game and everybody cries. You can't believe it's over. Then another team comes right behind you and you're forgotten."

"It was so long ago."

"Fifteen years, pal. When I was in college, I would come home for the holidays and stay away from this place. I wouldn't even drive by the school. Never saw Rake, didn't want to. Then one night in the summertime, right before I went back to college, just a month or so before they fired him, I bought a six-pack and climbed up here and replayed all the games. Stayed for hours. I could see us out there scoring at will, kicking ass every game. It was wonderful. Then it hurt like hell because it was over, our glory days gone in a flash."

"Did you hate Rake that night?"

"No, I loved him then."

"It changed every day."

"For most of us."

"Does it hurt now?"

"Not anymore. After I got married, we bought season tickets, joined the booster club, the usual stuff that everybody else does. Over time, I forgot about being a hero and became just another fan."

"You come to all the games?"

Paul pointed down to the left. "Sure. The bank owns a whole block of seats."

"You need a whole block with your family."

"Mona is very fertile."

"Evidently. How does she look?"

"She looks pregnant."

"I mean, you know, is she in shape?"

"Other words, is she fat?"

"That's it."

"No, she exercises two hours a day and eats only lettuce. She looks great and she'll want you over for dinner tonight."

"For lettuce?"

"For whatever you want. Can I call her?"

"No, not yet. Let's just talk."

There was no talk for a long time. They watched a pickup truck roll to a stop near the gate. The driver was a heavyset man with faded jeans, a denim cap, a thick beard, and a limp. He walked around the end zone and down the track and as he stepped up to the bleachers he noticed Neely and Curry sitting higher, watching every move he made. He nodded at them, climbed a few rows, then sat and gazed at the field, very still and very alone.

"That's Orley Short," Paul said, finally putting a name with a face. "Late seventies."

"I remember him," Neely said. "Slowest linebacker in history."

"And the meanest. All-conference, I think. Played one year at a juco then quit to cut timber for the rest of his life."

"Rake loved the loggers, didn't he?"

"Didn't we all? Four loggers on defense and a conference title was automatic."

Another pickup stopped near the first, another hefty gentleman in overalls and denim lumbered his way to the bleachers where he greeted Orley Short and sat beside him. Their meeting did not appear to be planned.

"Can't place him," Paul said, struggling to identify the second man and frustrated that he could not. In three and a half decades Rake had coached hundreds of boys from Messina and the county. Most of them had never left. Rake's players knew each other. They were members of a small fraternity whose membership was forever closed.

"You should get back more often," Paul said when it was time to talk again.

"Why?"

"Folks would like to see you."

"Maybe I don't want to see them."

"Why not?"

"I don't know."

"You think people here still hold a grudge because you didn't win the Heisman?"

"No."

"They'll remember you all right, but you're history. You're still their all-American, but that was a long time ago. Walk in Renfrow's Café and Maggie still has that huge photo of you above the cash register. I go there for breakfast every Thursday and sooner or later two old-timers will start debating who was the greatest Messina quarterback, Neely Crenshaw or Wally Webb. Webb started for four years, won forty-six in a row, never lost, etc., etc. But Crenshaw played against black kids and the game was faster and tougher. Crenshaw signed with Tech but Webb was too small for the big-time. They'll argue forever. They still love you, Neely."

"Thanks, but I'll skip it."

19

"Whatever."

"It was another life."

"Come on, give it up. Enjoy the memories."

"I can't. Rake's back there."

"Then why are you here?"

"I don't know."

A telephone buzzed from somewhere deep in Paul's nice dark suit. He found it and said, "Curry." A pause. "I'm at the field, with Crenshaw." A pause. "Yep, he's here. I swear. Okay." Paul slapped the phone shut and tucked it into a pocket.

"That was Silo," he said. "I told him you might be coming."

Neely smiled and shook his head at the thought of Silo Mooney. "I haven't seen him since we graduated."

"He didn't graduate, if you recall."

"Oh, yeah. I forgot."

"Had that little problem with the police. Schedule Four controlled substances. His father kicked him out of the house a month before we graduated."

"Now I remember."

"He lived in Rake's basement for a few weeks, then joined the Army."

"What's he doing now?"

"Well, let's say he's in the midst of a very colorful career. He left the Army with a dishonorable discharge, bounced around for a few years offshore on the rigs, got tired of honest work, and came back to Messina where he peddled drugs until he got shot at."

"I assume the bullet missed."

"By an inch, and Silo tried to go straight. I loaned him five thousand dollars to buy the old Franklin's Shoe Store and he set himself up as an entrepreneur. He cut the prices of his shoes while at the same time doubling his employees' wages, and went broke within a year. He sold cemetery lots, then used cars, then mobile homes. I lost track of him for a while. One day he walked into the bank and paid back everything he owed, in cash, said he'd finally struck gold."

"In Messina?"

"Yep. Somehow he swindled old man Joslin out of his junkyard, east of town. He fixed up a warehouse, and in the front half he runs a legitimate body shop. A cash cow. In the back half he runs a chop shop, specializing in stolen pickups. A real cash cow."

"He didn't tell you this."

"No, he didn't mention the chop shop. But I do his banking, and secrets are hard to keep around here. He's got some deal with a gang of thieves in the Carolinas whereby they ship him stolen trucks. He breaks them down and moves the parts. It's all cash, and evidently there's plenty of it."

"The cops?"

"Not yet, but everybody who deals with him is very careful. I expect the FBI to walk in any day with a subpoena, so I'm ready."

"Sounds just like Silo," Neely said.

"He's a mess. Drinks heavily, lots of women, throws cash around everywhere. Looks ten years older."

"Why am I not surprised? Does he still fight?"

"All the time. Be careful what you say about Rake. Nobody loves him like Silo. He'll come after you."

"Don't worry."

As the center on offense and the noseguard

on defense, Silo Mooney owned the middle of every field he played on. He was just under six feet tall with a physique that resembled, well, a silo: everything was thick—chest, waist, legs, arms. With Neely and Paul, he started for three years. Unlike the other two, Silo averaged three personal fouls in every game. Once he had four, one in each quarter. Twice he got ejected for kicking opposing linemen in the crotch. He lived for the sight of blood on the poor boy lined up against him. "Got that sumbitch bleedin' now," he would growl in the huddle, usually late in the first half. "He won't finish the game."

"Go ahead and kill him," Neely would say, egging on a mad dog. One less defensive lineman made Neely's job much easier.

No Messina player had ever been cursed by Coach Rake with as much frequency and enthusiasm as Silo Mooney. No one had deserved it as much. No one craved the verbal abuse as much as Silo.

At the north end of the bleachers, down where the rowdies from the county once raised so much hell, an older man moved quietly up to the top row and sat down. He was too far away to be recognized, and he certainly wanted to be alone. He gazed at the field, and was soon lost in his own memories.

The first jogger appeared and began plodding counterclockwise around the track. It was the time of day when the runners and walkers drifted to the field for a few laps. Rake had never allowed such nonsense, but after he was sacked a movement arose to open the track to the people who'd paid for it. A maintenance man was usually loitering somewhere nearby, watching to make sure no one dared step on the grass of Rake Field. There was no chance of that.

"Where's Floyd?" Neely asked.

"Still in Nashville picking his guitar and writing bad music. Chasing the dream."

"Ontario?"

"He's here, working at the post office. He and Takita have three kids. She's teaching school and as sweet as always. They're in church five times a week."

"So he's still smiling?"

"Always."

"Denny?"

"Still here, teaches chemistry in that building right over there. Never misses a game."

"Did you take chemistry?"

"I did not."

"Neither did I. I had straight A's and never cracked a book."

"You didn't have to. You were the all-American."

"And Jesse's still in jail?"

"Oh yeah, he'll be there for a long time."

"Where is he?"

"Buford. I see his mother every now and then and I always ask about him. It makes her cry but I can't help it."

"Wonder if he knows about Rake?" Neely said.

Paul shrugged and shook his head, and there was another gap in the conversation as they watched an old man struggle in a painful trot along the track. He was followed by two large young women, both burning more energy talking than walking.

"Did you ever learn the true story of why Jesse signed with Miami?" Neely asked.

"Not really. Lots of rumors about money, but Jesse would never say."

"Remember Rake's reaction?"

"Yeah, he wanted to kill Jesse. I think Rake had made some promises to the recruiter from A&M."

"Rake always wanted to deliver the prizes," Neely said, with an air of experience. "He wanted me at State."

"That's where you should've gone."

"Too late for that."

"Why'd you sign with Tech?"

"I liked their quarterback Coach."

"No one liked their quarterback Coach. What was the real reason?"

"You really want to know?"

"Yes, after fifteen years, I really want to know."

"Fifty thousand bucks in cash."

"No."

"Yep. State offered forty, A&M offered thirty-five, a few others were willing to pay twenty."

"You never told me that."

"I never told anyone until now. It's such a sleazy business."

"You took fifty thousand dollars in cash from Tech?" Paul asked slowly.

"Five hundred one-hundred-dollar bills, stuffed in an unmarked red canvas bag and placed in the trunk of my car one night while I was at the movies with Screamer. Next morning, I committed to Tech."

"Did your parents know?"

"Are you crazy? My father would've called the NCAA."

"Why'd you take it?"

"Every school offered cash, Paul, don't be naïve. It was part of the game."

"I'm not naïve, I'm just surprised at you."

"Why? I could've signed with Tech for nothing, or I could've taken the money. Fifty thousand bucks to an eighteen-year-old idiot is like winning the lottery."

"But still—"

"Every recruiter offered cash, Paul. There wasn't a single exception. I figured it was just part of the business."

"How'd you hide the money?"

"Stuffed it here and there. When I got to Tech, I paid cash for a new car. It didn't last long."

"And your parents weren't suspicious?"

"They were, but I was away at college and they couldn't keep up with everything."

"You saved none of it?"

"Why save money when you're on the pay-roll?"

"What payroll?"

Neely reshifted his weight and gave an indulging smile.

"Don't patronize me, asshole," Paul said. "Oddly enough most of us didn't play football at the Division One level."

"Remember the Gator Bowl my freshman year?"

"Sure. Everyone here watched it."

"I came off the bench in the second half, threw three touchdowns, ran for a hundred yards, won the game on a last-second pass. A star is born, I'm the greatest freshman in the country, blah, blah, blah. Well, when I got back to school there was a small package in my P.O. box. Five thousand bucks in cash. The note said: 'Nice game. Keep it up.' It was anonymous. The message was clear—keep winning and the money will keep coming. So I wasn't interested in saving money."

Silo's pickup had a custom paint job that was an odd mix between gold and red. The wheels glistened with silver and the windows were pitch black. "There he is," Paul said as the truck rolled to a stop near the gate.

"What kind of truck is that?" Neely asked.

"Stolen I'm sure."

Silo himself had been customized—a leather WWII bomber jacket, black denim pants, black boots. He hadn't lost weight, hadn't gained any either, and still looked like a nose tackle as he walked slowly around the edge of the field. It was the walk of a Messina Spartan, almost a strut, almost a challenge to anyone to utter a careless word. Silo could still put on the pads, snap the ball, and draw blood.

Instead he gazed at something in the middle of the field, perhaps it was himself a long time ago, perhaps he heard Rake barking at him. Whatever Silo heard or saw stopped him on the sideline for a moment, then he climbed the steps with his hands stuck deep in the pockets of his jacket. He was breathing hard when he got to Neely. He bearhugged his quarterback and asked him where he'd been for the past fifteen years. Greetings were exchanged, insults swapped. There was so much ground to cover that neither wanted to begin.

They sat three in a row and watched another jogger limp by. Silo was subdued, and when he spoke it was almost in a whisper. "So where are you living these days?"

"The Orlando area," Neely said.

"What kind of work you in?"

"Real estate."

"You got a family?"

"No, just one divorce. You?"

"Oh, I'm sure I got lots of kids, I just don't know about 'em. Never married. You makin' money?"

"Getting by. I'm not on the Forbes list."

"I'll probably crack it next year," Silo said.

"What kind of business?" Neely asked, glancing down at Paul.

"Automotive parts," Silo said. "I stopped by Rake's this afternoon. Miss Lila and the girls are there, along with the grandkids and neighbors. House is full of folks, all sittin' around, just waitin' for Rake to die."

"Did you see him?" Paul asked.

"No. He's somewhere in the back, with a nurse. Miss Lila said he didn't want anybody to see him in his last days. Said he's just a skeleton."

The image of Eddie Rake lying in a dark bed with a nurse nearby counting the minutes chilled the conversation for a long time. Until the day he was fired he coached in cleats and shorts and never hesitated to demonstrate the proper blocking mechanics or the finer points of a stiff arm. Rake relished physical contact with his players, but not the slap on the back for a job well done. Rake liked to hit, and no practice session was complete until he angrily threw down his clipboard and grabbed someone by the shoulder pads. The bigger the better. In blocking drills, when things were not going to suit him, he would crouch in a perfect three-point stance then fire off the ball and crash into a defensive tackle, one with forty more pounds and the full complement of pads and gear. Every Messina player had seen Rake, on a particularly bad day, throw his body at a running back and take him down with a vicious hit. He loved the violence of football and demanded it from every player.

In thirty-four years as head Coach, Rake had struck only two players off the field. The first had been a famous fistfight in the late sixties between the Coach and a hothead who had quit the team and was looking for trouble, of which he found plenty with Rake. The second had been a cheap shot that landed in the face of Neely Crenshaw.

It was incomprehensible that he was now a shriveled old man gasping for his last breath.

"I was in the Philippines," Silo said at low volume, but his voice was coarse and carried through the clear air. "I was guardin' toilets for the officers, hatin' every minute of it, and I never saw you play in college."

"You didn't miss much," Neely said.

"I heard later that you were great, then you got hurt."

"I had some nice games."

"He was the national player of the week when he was a sophomore," Paul said. "Threw for six touchdowns against Purdue."

"It was a knee, right?" Silo asked.

"Yes."

"How'd it happen?"

"I rolled out, into the flat, saw an opening,

tucked the ball and ran, didn't see a linebacker." Neely delivered the narrative as if he'd done it a thousand times and preferred not to do it again.

Silo had torn an ACL in spring football and survived it. He knew something about the knee. "Surgery and all that?" he asked.

"Four of them," Neely said. "Completely ruptured the ligament, busted the kneecap."

"So the helmet got you?"

"The linebacker went for the knee as Neely was stepping out of bounds," Paul said. "They showed it a dozen times on television. One of the announcers had the guts to call it a cheap shot. It was A&M, what can I say?"

"Must've hurt like hell."

"It did."

"He was carried off in an ambulance and they wept in the streets of Messina."

"I'm sure that's true," Silo said. "But it doesn't take much to get this town upset. Rehab didn't work?"

"It was what they sadly refer to as a career-ending injury," Neely said. "Therapy made things worse. I was toast from the second I tucked the ball and ran. Should've stayed in the pocket like I'd been coached."

"Rake never told you to stay in the pocket."

"It's a different game up there, Silo."

"Yeah, they're a bunch of dumbasses. They never recruited me. I could've been great, probably the first nose tackle to win the Heisman."

"No doubt about it," Paul said.

"Everybody knew it at Tech," Neely said. "All the players kept asking me, 'Where's the great Silo Mooney? Why didn't we sign him?'"

"What a waste," Paul said. "You'd still be in the NFL."

"Probably with the Packers," Silo said. "Making the big bucks. Chicks bangin' on my door. The life."

"Didn't Rake want you to go to a junior college?" Neely asked.

"Yeah, I was headed there, but they wouldn't let me finish school here."

"How'd you get in the Army?"

"I lied."

And there was no doubt that Silo had lied to get in the Army, and probably lied to get out. "I need a beer," he said. "You guys want a beer?"

"I'll pass," Paul said. "I need to be heading home soon."

"What about you?"

"A beer would be nice," Neely said.

"You gonna stay here for a while?" Silo asked.

"Maybe."

"Me too. It just seems like the place to be right now."

———

The Spartan Marathon was an annual torture run created by Rake to inaugurate each season. It was held the first day of August practice, always at noon, for maximum heat. Every varsity hopeful reported to the track in gym shorts and running shoes, and when Rake blew his whistle the laps began.

The format was simple—you ran until you dropped. Twelve laps were the minimum. Any player unable to complete twelve laps would get the chance to repeat the marathon the next day, and if he failed twice then he was unfit to become a Messina Spartan. Any high school football player who could not run three miles had no business putting on the pads.

The assistant coaches sat in the air-conditioned press box and counted laps. Rake prowled from one end zone to the other watching the runners, barking if necessary, disqualifying those who moved too slow. Speed was not an issue, unless a player's pace became a walk, at which point Rake would pull him off the track. Once a player quit or passed out or was otherwise disqualified, he was forced to sit at midfield and bake under the sun until there was no one left standing. There were very few rules, one of which called for automatic ejection if a runner vomited on the track. Vomiting was allowed and there was plenty of it, but once it was completed, somewhere off the track, the sick player was expected to rejoin the run.

Of Rake's vast repertoire of harsh conditioning methods, the marathon was by far the most dreaded. Over the years it had led some young men in Messina to pursue other sports, or to leave athletics altogether. Mention it to a player around town in July and he suddenly had a thick knot in his stomach and a dry mouth. By early August, most players were running at least five miles a day in anticipation.

Because of the marathon, every Spartan reported in superb condition. It was not unusual for a hefty lineman to lose twenty or thirty pounds over the summer, not for his girlfriend and not for his physique. The weight was shed to survive the Spartan Marathon. Once it was over, the eating could start again, though weight was difficult to gain when you spent three hours a day on the practice field.

Coach Rake didn't like big linemen anyway. He preferred the nasty types like Silo Mooney.

Neely's senior year he completed thirty-one laps, almost eight miles, and when he fell onto the grass with the dry heaves he could hear Rake cursing him from across the field. Paul ran nine and a half miles that year, thirty-eight laps, and won the race. Every Spartan remembered two numbers—the one on his jersey, and the number of laps he finished in the Spartan Marathon.

After the knee injury had abruptly reduced him to the status of being just another student at Tech, Neely was in a bar when a coed from Messina spotted him. "Heard the news from home?" she said. "What news?" Neely asked, not the least bit interested in news from his hometown.

"Got a new record in the Spartan Marathon."

"Oh really."

"Yeah, eighty-three laps."

Neely repeated what she'd said, did the math, then said, "That's almost twenty-one miles."

"Yep."

"Who did it?"

"Some kid named Jaeger."

Only in Messina would the gossip include the latest stats from the August workouts.

Randy Jaeger was now climbing up the bleachers, wearing his green game jersey with the number 5 in white with silver trim, tucked tightly into his jeans. He was small, very thin at the waist, no doubt a wide receiver with quick feet and an impressive time in the forty. He first recognized Paul, and as he drew closer he saw Neely. He stopped three rows down and said, "Neely Crenshaw."

"That's me," Neely said. They shook hands. Paul knew Jaeger well because, as was established quickly in the conversation, Randy's family owned a shopping center north of town, and, like everybody else in Messina, they banked with Paul.

"Any word on Rake?" Jaeger asked, settling onto the row behind and leaning forward between them.

"Not much. He's still hanging on," Paul said gravely.

"When did you finish?" Neely asked.

"Ninety-three."

"And they fired him in—"

"Ninety-two, my senior year. I was one of the captains."

There was a heavy pause as the story of Rake's termination came and went without comment. Neely had been drifting through western Canada, in a post-college funk that lasted almost five years, and had missed the drama. Over time, he had heard some of the details, though he had tried to convince himself he didn't care what happened to Eddie Rake.

"You ran the eighty-three laps?" Neely asked.

"Yep, in 1990, when I was a sophomore."

"Still the record?"

"Yep. You?"

"Thirty-one, my senior year. Eighty-three is hard to believe."

"I got lucky. It was cloudy and cool."

"How about the guy who came in second?"

"Forty-five, I think."

"Doesn't sound like luck to me. Did you play in college?"

"No, I weighed one-thirty with pads on."

"He was all-state for two years," Paul said. "And still holds the record for return yardage. His momma just couldn't fatten him up."

"I got a question," Neely said. "I ran thirty-one laps and collapsed in pain. Then Rake cussed me like a dog. What, exactly, did he say when you finished with eighty-three?"

Paul grunted and grinned because he'd heard the story. Jaeger shook his head and smiled. "Typical Rake," he said. "When I finished, he walked by me and said, in a loud voice, 'I thought you could do a hundred.' Of course, this was for the benefit of the other players. Later, in the locker room, he said, very quietly, that it was a gutsy performance."

Two of the joggers left the track and walked up a few rows where they sat by themselves and stared at the field. They were in their early fifties, tanned and fit with expensive running shoes. "Guy on the right is Blanchard Teague," Paul said, anxious to prove he knew everyone. "Our optometrist. On the left is Jon Couch, a lawyer. They played in the late sixties, during The Streak."

"So they never lost a game," Jaeger said.

"That's right. In fact, the '68 team was never scored on. Twelve games, twelve shutouts. Those two guys were there."

"Awesome," Jaeger said, truly in awe.

"That was before we were born," Paul said.

A scoreless season took a minute to digest. The optometrist and the lawyer were deep in conversation, no doubt replaying their glorious achievements during The Streak.

"The paper did a story on Rake a few years after he was fired," Paul said softly. "It ran all the usual stats, but also added that in thirty-four years he coached seven hundred and fourteen players. That was the title of the story—'Eddie Rake and the Seven Hundred Spartans.'"

"I saw that," Jaeger said.

"I wonder how many will be at his funeral?" Paul said.

"Most of them."

Silo's version of a beverage run included the gathering of two cases of beer and two other guys to help drink it. Three men emerged from his pickup, with Silo leading the way, a box of Budweiser on his shoulder. One bottle was in his hand.

"Oh boy," Paul said.

"Who's the skinny guy?" Neely asked.

"I think it's Hubcap."

"Hubcap's not in jail?"

"He comes and goes."

"The other one is Amos Kelso," Jaeger said. "He played with me."

Amos was hauling the other case of beer, and as the three stomped up the bleachers Silo invited Orley Short and his pal to join them for a drink. They did not hesitate. He yelled at Teague and Couch, and they too followed them up to row thirty, where Neely and Paul and Randy Jaeger were sitting.

Once the introductions were made and the

bottles were opened, Orley asked the group, "What's the latest on Rake?"

"Just waiting," Paul said.

"I stopped by this afternoon," Couch said gravely. "It's just a matter of time." Couch had an air of lawyerly importance that Neely immediately disliked. Teague the optometrist then provided a lengthy narrative about the latest advances of Rake's cancer.

It was almost dark. The joggers were gone from the track. In the shadows a tall gawky man emerged from the clubhouse and slowly made his way to the metal poles supporting the scoreboard.

"That's not Rabbit, is it?" Neely asked.

"Of course it is," Paul said. "He'll never leave."

"What's his title now?"

"He doesn't need one."

"He taught me history," Teague said.

"And he taught me math," Couch said.

Rabbit had taught for eleven years before someone discovered he'd never finished the ninth grade. He was fired in the ensuing scandal, but Rake intervened and got Rabbit reassigned as an assistant athletic director. Such a title at Messina High School meant he did nothing but take orders from Rake. He drove the team bus, cleaned uniforms, maintained equipment, and, most important, supplied Rake with all the gossip.

The field lights were mounted on four poles, two on each side. Rabbit flipped a switch. The lights on the south end of the visitors' side came on, ten rows of ten lights each. Long shadows fell across the field.

"Been doing that for a week now," Paul said. "Rabbit leaves them on all night. His version of a vigil. When Rake dies, the lights go out."

Rabbit lurched and wobbled back to the clubhouse, gone for the night. "Does he still live there?" Neely asked.

"Yep. He has a cot in the attic, above the weight room. Calls himself a night watchman. He's crazy as hell."

"He was a damned good math teacher," Couch said.

"He's lucky he can still walk," Paul said, and everyone laughed. Rabbit had become partially crippled during a game in 1981 when, for reasons neither he nor anyone else would ever grasp, he had sprinted from the sideline onto the field, into the path of one Lightning Loyd, a fast and rugged running back, who later played at Auburn, but who, on that night, was playing for Greene County, and playing quite brilliantly. With the score tied late in the third quarter, Loyd broke free for what appeared to be a long touchdown run. Both teams were undefeated. The game was tense, and evidently Rabbit snapped under the pressure. To the horror (and delight) of ten thousand Messina faithful, Rabbit flung his bony and brittle body into the arena, and somewhere around the thirty-five-yard line, he collided with Lightning. The collision, while near fatal for Rabbit, who at the time was at least forty years old, had little impact on Loyd. A bug on the windshield.

Rabbit was wearing khakis, a green Messina sweatshirt, a green cap that shot skyward and came to rest ten yards away, and a pair of pointed-toe cowboy boots, the left one of which was jolted free and spun loose while Rabbit was airborne. People sitting thirty rows up swore they heard Rabbit's bones break.

If Lightning had continued his sprint, the controversy would have been lessened considerably. But the poor kid was so shocked that he glanced over his shoulder to see who and what he had just run over, and in doing so lost his balance. It took fifteen yards for him to complete his fall, and when he came to rest somewhere around the twenty-yard line the field was covered with yellow flags.

While the trainers huddled over Rabbit and debated whether to call for an ambulance or a minister, the officials quickly awarded the touchdown to Greene County, a decision that Rake argued with for a moment then conceded. Rake was as shocked as anyone, and he was also concerned about Rabbit, who hadn't moved a muscle since hitting the ground.

It took twenty minutes to gather Rabbit up and place him gently on the stretcher and shove him into an ambulance. As it drove away, ten thousand Messina fans stood and applauded with respect. The folks from Greene County, uncertain as to whether they too should applaud or boo, just sat quietly and tried to digest what they had seen. They had their touchdown, but the poor idiot appeared to be dead.

Rake, always the master motivator, used the delay to incite his troops. "Rabbit's hittin' harder than you clowns," he growled at his defense. "Let's kick some ass and take the game ball to Rabbit!"

Messina scored three touchdowns in the fourth quarter and won easily.

Rabbit survived too. His collarbone was broken and three lower veterbrae were cracked. His concussion was not severe, and those who knew him well claimed they noticed no additional brain damage. Needless to say, Rabbit became a local hero. At the annual football banquet thereafter Rake awarded a Rabbit Trophy for the Hit-of-the-Year.

The lights grew brighter as dusk came to an end. Their eyes refocused in the semi-lit darkness of Rake Field. Another, smaller group of old Spartans had materialized at the far end of the bleachers. Their voices were barely audible.

Silo opened another bottle and drained half of it.

"When was the last time you saw Rake?" Blanchard Teague asked Neely.

"A couple of days after my first surgery," Neely said, and everyone was still. He was telling a story that had never been told before in Messina. "I was in the hospital. One surgery down, three to go."

"It was a cheap shot," Couch mumbled, as if Neely needed to be reassured.

"Damned sure was," said Amos Kelso.

Neely could see them, huddled in the coffee shops on Main Street, long sad faces, low grave voices as they replayed the late hit that instantly ruined the career of their all-American. A nurse told him she had never seen such an outpouring of compassion—cards, flowers, chocolates, balloons, artwork from entire classes of grade-schoolers. All from the small town of Messina, three hours away. Other than his parents and the Tech coaches, Neely refused all visitors. For eight long days he drowned himself in pity, aided mightily by as many painkillers as the doctors would allow.

Rake slipped in one night, long after visiting hours were over. "He tried to cheer me up,"

Neely said, sipping a beer. "Said knees could be rehabbed. I tried to believe him."

"Did he mention the '87 championship game?" Silo asked.

"We talked about it."

There was a long awkward pause as they contemplated that game, and all the mysteries around it. It was Messina's last title, and that alone was a source rich enough for years of analysis. Down 31–0 at the half, roughed up and manhandled by a vastly superior team from East Pike, the Spartans returned to the field at A&M where thirty-five thousand fans were waiting. Rake was absent; he didn't appear until late in the fourth quarter.

The truth about what happened had remained buried for fifteen years, and, evidently, neither Neely, nor Silo, nor Paul, nor Hubcap Taylor were about to break the silence.

In the hospital room Rake had finally apologized, but Neely had told no one.

Teague and Couch said good-bye and jogged away in the darkness.

"You never came back, did you?" Jaeger asked.

"Not after I got hurt," Neely said.

"Why not?"

"Didn't want to."

Hubcap had been working quietly on a pint of something much stronger than beer. He'd said little, and when he spoke his tongue was thick. "People say you hated Rake."

"That's not true."

"And he hated you."

"Rake had a problem with the stars," Paul said. "We all knew that. If you won too many awards, set too many records, Rake got jealous. Plain and simple. He worked us like dogs and wanted every one of us to be great, but when guys like Neely got all the attention then Rake got envious."

"I don't believe that," Orley Short grunted.

"It's true. Plus he wanted to deliver the prizes to whatever college he happened to like at the moment. He wanted Neely at State."

"He wanted me in the Army," Silo said.

"Lucky you didn't go to prison," Paul said.

"It ain't over yet," Silo said with a laugh.

Another car rolled to a stop by the gate and its headlights went off. No door opened.

"Prison's underrated," Hubcap said, and everyone laughed.

"Rake had his favorites," Neely said. "I wasn't one of them."

"Then why are you here?" asked Orley Short.

"I'm not sure. Same reason you're here, I guess."

During Neely's freshman year at Tech, he had returned for Messina's homecoming game. In a halftime ceremony, they retired number 19. The standing ovation went on and on and eventually delayed the second half kickoff, which cost the Spartans five yards and prompted Coach Rake, leading 28–0, to start yelling.

That was the only game Neely had watched since he left. One year later he was in the hospital.

"When did they put up Rake's bronze statue?" he asked.

"Couple of years after they fired him," Jaeger said. "The boosters raised ten thousand bucks and had it done. They wanted to present it to him before a game, but he refused."

"So he never came back?"

"Well, sort of." Jaeger pointed to a hill in the

distance behind the clubhouse. "He'd drive up on Karr's Hill before every game and park on one of those gravel roads. He and Miss Lila would sit there, looking down, listening to Buck Coffey on the radio, too far away to see much, but making sure the town knew he was still watching. At the end of every halftime the band would face the hill and play the fight song, and all ten thousand would wave at Rake."

"It was pretty cool," said Amos Kelso.

"Rake knew everything that was going on," Paul said. "Rabbit called him twice a day with the gossip."

"Was he a recluse?" Neely asked.

"He kept to himself," Amos said. "For the first three or four years anyway. There were rumors he was moving, but then rumors don't mean much here. He went to Mass every morning, but that's a small crowd in Messina."

"He got out more in the last few years," Paul said. "Started playing golf."

"Was he bitter?"

The question was pondered by the rest of them. "Yeah, he was bitter," said Jaeger.

"I don't think so," Paul said. "He blamed himself."

"Rumor has it that they'll bury him next to Scotty," Amos said.

"I heard that too," Silo said, very deep in thought.

A car door slammed and a figure stepped onto the track. A stocky man in a uniform of some variety swaggered around the field and approached the bleachers.

"Here's trouble," Amos mumbled.

"It's Mal Brown," Silo said softly.

"Our illustrious Sheriff," Paul said to Neely.

"Number 31?"

"That's him."

Neely's number 19 was the last jersey retired. Number 31 was the first. Mal Brown had played in the mid-sixties, during The Streak. Eighty pounds and thirty-five years ago he had been a bruising tailback who had once carried the ball fifty-four times in a game, still a Messina record. A quick marriage ended the college career before it began, and a quick divorce sent him to Vietnam in time for the Tet Offensive in '68. Neely had heard stories of the great Mal Brown throughout most of his childhood. Before a game Neely's freshman year, Coach Rake stopped by for a quick pep talk. He recounted in great detail how Mal Brown had once rushed for two hundred yards in the second half of the conference championship, and he did so with a broken ankle!

Rake loved stories of players who refused to leave the field with broken bones and bleeding flesh and all sorts of gruesome injuries.

Years later, Neely would hear that Mal's broken ankle had, more than likely, been a severe sprain, but as the years passed the legend grew, at least in Rake's memory.

The Sheriff walked along the front of the bleachers and spoke to the others passing the time, then he climbed thirty rows and arrived, almost gasping, at Neely's group. He spoke to Paul, then Amos, Silo, Orley, Hubcap, Randy—he knew them all by their first names or nicknames. "Heard you were in town," he said to Neely as they shook hands. "It's been a long time."

"It has" was all Neely could say. To his recollection, he had never met Mal Brown. He wasn't the Sheriff when Neely lived in Messina. Neely knew the legend, but not the man.

Didn't matter. They were fraternity brothers.

"It's dark, Silo, how come you ain't stealin' cars?" Mal said.

"Too early."

"I'm gonna bust your ass, you know that?"

"I got lawyers."

"Gimme a beer. I'm off duty." Silo handed over a beer and Mal slugged it down. "Just left Rake's," he said, smacking his lips as if he hadn't had liquids in days. "Nothing's changed. Just waitin' for him to go."

The update was received without comment.

"Where you been hidin'?" Mal asked Neely.

"Nowhere."

"Don't lie. Nobody's seen you here in ten years, maybe longer."

"My parents retired to Florida. I had no reason to come back."

"This is where you grew up. It's home. Ain't that a reason?"

"Maybe for you."

"Maybe my ass. You got a lot of friends around here. Ain't right to run away."

"Drink another beer, Mal," Paul said.

Silo quickly passed another one down, and

Mal grabbed it. After a minute, he said, "You got kids?"

"No."

"How's your knee?"

"It's ruined."

"Sorry." A long drink. "What a cheap shot. You were clearly out of bounds."

"I should've stayed in the pocket," Neely said, shifting his weight, wishing he could change the subject. How long would the town of Messina talk about the cheap shot that ruined his career?

Another long drink, then Mal said softly, "Man, you were the greatest."

"Let's talk about something else," Neely said. He'd been there for almost three hours and was suddenly anxious to leave, though he had no idea where he might be going. Two hours earlier there had been talk of Mona Curry cooking dinner, but that offer had not been pursued.

"Okay, what?"

"Let's talk about Rake," Neely said. "What was his worst team?"

All bottles rose at once as the group contemplated this.

Mal spoke first. "He lost four games in '76. Miss Lila swears he went into solitary confinement for the winter. Stopped goin' to Mass. Refused to be seen in public. He put the team on a brutal conditionin' program, ran 'em like dogs all summer, made 'em practice three times a day in August. But when they kicked off in '77 it was a different team. Almost won state."

"How could Rake lose four games in one season?" Neely asked.

Mal leaned back and rested on the row behind him. Took a swig. He was by far the oldest Spartan present, and since he hadn't missed a game in thirty years he had the floor. "Well, first of all, the team had absolutely no talent. The price of timber shot up in the summer of '76, and all the loggers quit. You know how they are. Then the quarterback broke his arm, and there was no backup. We played Harrisburg that year and never threw a pass. Makes it tough when they're sendin' all eleven on every play. It was a disaster."

"Harrisburg beat us?" Neely asked in disbelief.

"Yep, the only time in the past forty-one

years. And lemme tell you what those dumb sumbitches did. They're leadin' late in the game, big score, somethin' like thirty-six to nothin'. The worst night in the history of Messina football. So they figure they've turned the corner in their sad little rivalry with us, and they decide to run up the score. With a coupla minutes to go, they throw a reverse pass on third and short. Another touchdown. They're real excited, you know, they're stickin' it to the Messina Spartans. Rake kept his cool, wrote it down somewhere in blood, and went lookin' for loggers. Next year, we're playin' Harrisburg here, huge crowd, angry crowd, we score seven touchdowns in the first half."

"I remember that game," Paul said. "I was in the first grade. Forty-eight to nothing."

"Forty-seven," Mal said proudly. "We scored four times in the third quarter, and Rake kept passin'. He couldn't sub because he had no bench, but he kept the ball in the air."

"The final?" Neely asked.

"Ninety-four to nothin'. Still a Messina record. The only time I've ever known Eddie Rake to run up a score."

The other group on the north end erupted in laughter as someone finished a story, no doubt about Rake or some long-ago game. Silo had become very quiet in the presence of the law, and when the moment was right he said, "Well, I need to be going. Call me, Curry, if you hear something about Rake."

"I will."

"See y'all tomorrow," Silo said, standing, stretching, reaching for one last bottle.

"I need a ride," Hubcap said.

"It's that time of the night, huh, Silo?" Mal said. "Time for all good thieves to ease out of the gutter."

"I'm laying off for a few days," Silo said. "In honor of Coach Rake."

"How touchin'. I'll just send the night shift boys home then, since you're closin' shop."

"You do that, Mal."

Silo, Hubcap, and Amos Kelso lumbered down the bleachers, the metal steps rattling as they descended.

"He'll be in prison within twelve months," Mal said as they watched them walk along the track behind the end zone. "Make sure your bank is clean, Curry."

"Don't worry."

Neely had heard enough. He stood and said, "I'll be running along too."

"I thought you were coming to dinner," Paul said.

"I'm not hungry now. How about tomorrow night?"

"Mona will be disappointed."

"Tell her to save the leftovers. Good night, Mal, Randy. I'm sure I'll see you soon."

The knee was stiff, and as Neely crept down the steps he tried mightily to do so without a limp, without a hint that he was anything less than what they remembered. On the track, behind the Spartan bench, he turned too quickly and the knee almost collapsed. It buckled, then wavered as tiny sharp pains hit in a dozen different spots. Because it happened so often, he knew how to lift it just so and quickly shift all weight to his right leg, and to keep walking as if everything was normal.

their coffee, but he kept moving toward a booth by the window. Neely nodded and tried to avoid eye contact. By the time they slid into their seats, the secret was out. Neely Crenshaw was indeed back in town.

The walls were covered with old football schedules, framed newspaper stories, pennants, autographed jerseys, and hundreds of photos— team photos lined in neat chronological order above the counter, action shots lifted from the local paper, and large black-and-whites of the greatest of Spartans. Neely's was above the cash register, a photo of him as a senior, posing with the football cocked and ready to fire, no helmet, no smile, all business and attitude and ego, long untamed hair, three days' worth of stubble and peach fuzz, eyes looking somewhere in the distance, no doubt dreaming of future glory.

"You were so cute back then," Paul said.

"Seems like yesterday, then it seems like a dream."

In the center of the longest wall there was a shrine to Eddie Rake—a large color photo of him standing near the goalposts, and under it the record—418 wins, 62 losses, 13 state titles.

According to the predawn gossip, Rake was still clinging to life. And the town was still clinging to him. The chatter was subdued—no laughter, no jokes, no windy stories of fishing triumphs, none of the usual spats over politics.

A tiny waitress in a green-and-white outfit brought them coffee and took their orders. She knew Paul but did not recognize the guy with him.

"Is Maggie still around?" Neely asked.

"Nursing home," Paul said.

Maggie Renfrow had been serving scalded coffee and oily eggs for decades. She had also dealt relentlessly in all areas of gossip and rumor surrounding the Spartan football team. Because she had given free meals to the players she had managed to do what everyone else in Messina tried to do—wiggle in a little closer to the boys and their Coach.

A gentleman approached and nodded awkwardly at Neely. "Just wanted to say hello," he said, easing out his right hand. "Good to see you again, after all this time. You were something."

Neely shook his hand and said, "Thanks." The handshake was brief. Neely broke eye contact. The gentleman took the hint and withdrew. No one followed him.

There were quick glances and awkward stares, but the others seemed content to brood over the coffee and ignore him. After all, he had ignored them for the past fifteen years. Messina owned its heroes, and they were expected to enjoy the nostalgia.

"When was the last time you saw Screamer?" Paul asked.

Neely snorted and looked out of the window. "I haven't seen her since college."

"Not a word?"

"One letter, years back. Fancy stationery from some place in Hollywood. Said she was taking the place by storm. Said she'd be a lot more famous than I ever thought about being. Pretty nasty stuff. I didn't respond."

"She showed up for our ten-year reunion," Paul said. "An actress, nothing but blond hair and legs, outfits that have never been seen around here. A pretty elaborate production. Name-dropping right and left, this producer, that director, a bunch of actors I'd never heard of. I got the impression she was spending more time in bed than in front of the camera."

"That's Screamer."

"You should know."

"How'd she look?"

"Tired."

"Any credits?"

"Quite a few, and they changed by the hour. We compared notes later, and no one had seen anything she said she'd been in. It was all a show. Typical Screamer. Except that now she's Tessa. Tessa Canyon."

"Tessa Canyon?"

"Yep."

"Sounds like a porn star."

"I think that's where she was headed."

"Poor girl."

"Poor girl?" Paul repeated. "She's a miserable self-absorbed idiot whose only claim to fame was that she was Neely Crenshaw's girlfriend."

"Yes, but those legs."

They both smiled for a long time. The waitress brought their pancakes and sausage and refilled their coffees. As Paul drenched his plate with maple syrup, he began talking again. "Two years ago, we had a big bankers' convention in Vegas. Mona was with me. She got bored, went to the room. I got bored, so I walked along the Strip, late at night. I ducked into one of the older casinos, and guess who I saw?"

"Tessa Canyon."

"Tessa was shuffling booze, a cocktail waitress in one of those tight little costumes that's low in the front and high in the rear. Bleached hair, thick makeup, twenty or so extra pounds. She didn't see me so I watched her for a few minutes. She looked older than thirty. The odd thing was how she performed. When she got near her customers at the tables, the smile came on with the purring little voice that says, 'Take me upstairs.' The glib one-liners. The bumping and rubbing. Shameless flirting with a bunch of drunks. The woman just wants to be loved."

"I tried my best."

"She's a sad case."

"That's why I dumped her. She won't come back for the funeral, will she?"

"Maybe. If there's a chance she'll bump into you, then yes, she'll be here. On the other hand, she ain't lookin' too good, and with Screamer looks are everything."

"Her parents are still here?"

"Yeah."

A chubby man wearing a John Deere cap eased to their table as if he was trespassing. "Just wanted to say hello, Neely," he said, almost ready to bow. "Tim Nunley, down at the Ford place," he said, offering a hand as if it might be ignored. Neely shook it and smiled. "Used to work on your daddy's cars."

"I remember you," Neely lied, but the lie was worth the effort. Mr. Nunley's smile doubled in size and he squeezed Neely's hand harder.

"I thought you would," Mr. Nunley said, glancing at his table for vindication. "Good to see you back here. You were the greatest."

"Thank you," Neely said, releasing his hand and grabbing a fork. Mr. Nunley backed away, still waiting to bow, then took his coat and left the restaurant.

The conversations were still muted around the tables, as if the wake had already begun. Paul finished a mouthful and leaned in low. "Four years ago we had a good team. Won the first nine games. Undefeated. I was sitting right here eating the same thing I'm eating now, on a Friday morning, game day, and, I swear this is true, the topic of conversation that morning was The Streak. Not the old streak, but a new one. These people were ready for a new streak. Never mind a winning season, or a conference title, or even a state championship, they're all peanuts. This town wants eighty, ninety, maybe a hundred wins in a row."

Neely looked around quickly then returned to his breakfast. "I've never understood it," he said. "These are nice folks—mechanics, truck drivers, insurance salesmen, builders, maybe a lawyer, maybe a banker. Solid small-town citizens, but not exactly earthshakers. I mean, nobody here is making a million bucks. But they're entitled to a state championship every year, right?"

"Right."

"I don't get it."

"Bragging rights. What else can they brag about?"

"No wonder they worship Rake. He put the town on the map."

"Take a bite," Paul said. A man with a dirty

apron approached holding a manila file. He introduced himself as Maggie Renfrow's brother, now the chef, and he opened the file. Inside was a framed eight by ten color photo of Neely at Tech. "Maggie always wanted you to sign this," he said.

It was a splendid picture of Neely in action, crouching behind the center, calling a play, ready for the snap, sizing up the defense. A purple helmet was visible in the right lower corner, and Neely realized the opponent was A&M. The photo, one he'd never seen before, was taken minutes before he was injured. "Sure," he said, taking a black marker from the chef.

He signed his name across the top, and for a long moment looked into the eyes of a young, fearless quarterback, a star biding his time in college while the NFL waited. He could hear the Tech crowd that day, seventy-five thousand strong and desperate for victory, proud of their undefeated team, thrilled that they, for the first time in many years, had a bona-fide all-American at quarterback.

Suddenly, he longed for those days.

"Nice photo," he managed to say, handing it

back to the chef, who took it and immediately hung it on a nail under the larger photo of Neely.

"Let's get outta here," Neely said, wiping his mouth. He placed some cash on the table, and they began a quick exit. He nodded, smiled politely at the regulars, and managed to make an escape without being stopped.

"Why are you so nervous around these folks?" Paul asked when they were outside.

"I don't want to talk about football, okay? I don't want to hear how great I was."

They drove the quiet streets around the square, passing the church where Neely was baptized, and the church where Paul was married, and the handsome split-level on Tenth Street where Neely lived from the age of eight until he left for Tech. His parents had sold it to a certified Yankee who'd been brought down to manage the paper mill west of town. They passed Rake's house, slowly, as if they might hear the latest just by driving down the street. The driveway was crowded with cars, most with out-of-state license plates, Rake's family and close friends, they figured. They passed the park where they'd played Little League baseball and Pop Warner football.

And they remembered stories. One that was now a legend in Messina was, of course, about Rake. Neely, Paul, and a handful of their buddies were playing a rowdy game of sandlot football when they noticed a man standing in the distance, near the backstop of the baseball field, watching them closely. When they finished, he ventured over and introduced himself as Coach Eddie Rake. The boys were speechless. "You have a nice arm, son," he said to Neely, who could say nothing in response. "I like your feet too."

All the boys looked at Neely's feet.

"Is your mother as tall as your father?" Coach Rake asked.

"Almost," Neely managed to say.

"Good. You'll make a great Spartan quarterback." Rake smiled at the boys, then walked away.

Neely was eleven years old at the time.

They stopped at the cemetery.

———

The approach of the 1992 season caused great concern in Messina. The year before the team had lost three games, a civic disaster that had them grumbling over their biscuits at Renfrow's and rubber chicken at the Rotary lunches and cheap beer at the tonks out in the county. And there had been few seniors on that team, always a bad sign. It was a relief when weak players graduated.

If Rake felt pressure, he certainly didn't show it. By then he'd been coaching the Spartans for more than three decades and had seen everything. His last state title, number thirteen, had been in 1987, so the locals were suffering through a three-year drought. They'd been through worse. They were spoiled and wanted a hundred wins in a row, and Rake, after thirty-four years, didn't care what they wanted.

The '92 team had little talent, and everyone knew it. The only star was Randy Jaeger, who played corner and wideout, where he caught anything the quarterback could throw near him, which was not very much.

In a town the size of Messina, the talent came in cycles. On the upswing, as in 1987 with Neely, Silo, Paul, Alonzo Taylor, and four vicious loggers on defense, the scores were lopsided. Rake's greatness, however, was winning with players who were small and slow. He took thin talent and still delivered scores that were lop-sided. He worked the lean ones harder, though, and few teams had seen the intensity that Rake brought to the field in August 1992.

After a bad scrimmage on a Saturday after-noon, Rake lashed out at the team and called a Sunday morning practice, something he rarely did because, in years past, it had upset the church folks. Eight o'clock Sunday morning, so that the boys would have time to attend worship, if they were able. Rake was particularly upset over what he perceived to be a lack of conditioning, a joke since every Messina team ran sprints by the hundreds.

Shorts, shoulder pads, gym shoes, helmets, no contact, just conditioning. It was eighty-nine degrees by eight o'clock, with thick humidity and a cloudless sky. They stretched and ran a mile around the track, just for a warm-up. Every player was soaked with sweat when Rake called for a second mile.

Number two on the list of dreaded tortures, just behind the Spartan Marathon, was the assault on the bleachers. Every player knew what it meant, and when Rake yelled, "Bleachers," half the team wanted to quit.

Following Randy Jaeger, their captain, the players formed a long, reluctant, single line and began a slow jog around the track. When the line approached the visitors' stands, Jaeger turned through a gate and started up the bleachers, twenty rows, then along the top rail, then down twenty rows to the next section. Eight sections on the other side, then back on the track, around the end zone to the home side. Fifty rows up, along the top rail, fifty rows down, up and down, up and down, up and down, for another eight sections, then back on the track for another loop.

After one grueling round, the linemen were drifting to the rear, and Jaeger, who could run forever, was far in front. Rake growled along the track, whistle hanging around his neck, yelling at the stragglers. He loved the sound of fifty players stomping up and down the bleachers. "You guys are not in shape," he said, just loud enough to be heard. "Slowest bunch I've ever seen," he grumbled, again, barely audible. Rake was famous for his grumbling, which could always be heard.

After the second round, a tackle fell to the

grass and began vomiting. The heavier players were moving slower and slower.

Scotty Reardon was a sophomore special-teams player who weighed in that August at 141 pounds, but, at the time of his autopsy, weighed 129. During the third round of bleachers, he collapsed between the third and fourth rows on the home side, and never regained consciousness.

Since it was Sunday morning, and a no-contact session, both team trainers were absent, at Rake's instructions. Nor was there an ambulance close by. The boys would describe later how Rake held Scotty's head in his lap while they waited for an eternity to hear a siren. But he was dead in the bleachers, and he was certainly dead when he finally arrived at the hospital. Heatstroke.

Paul was telling the story as they walked through the winding, shaded lanes of the Messina Cemetery. In a newer section, on the side of a steep hill, the headstones were smaller, the rows neater. He nodded at one and Neely knelt down for a look. Randall Scott Reardon. Born June 20, 1977. Died August 21, 1992.

"And they're going to bury him over there?"

Neely asked, pointing to a bare spot next to Scotty.

"That's the rumor," Paul said.

"This place is always good for a rumor."

They walked a few steps to a wrought-iron bench under a small elm tree, sat, and looked at Scotty's headstone. "Who had the guts to fire him?" Neely asked.

"The wrong kid died. Scotty's family had some money, from timber. His uncle, John Reardon, was elected Superintendent of Education in '89. Very highly regarded, smart as hell, smooth politician, and the only person with the authority to fire Eddie Rake. Fire him he did. The town, as you might guess, was shocked by the news of the death, and as the details came out there was some grumbling about Rake and his methods."

"Lucky he didn't kill all of us."

"An autopsy was done on Monday—a clear case of heatstroke. No preexisting conditions. No defects anywhere. A perfectly healthy fifteen-year-old leaves home at seven-thirty on a Sunday morning for a two-hour torture session, and he doesn't come home. For the first time in the history of this town people were asking, 'Why, exactly, do you run kids in a sauna until they puke?' "

"And the answer was?"

"Rake had no answers. Rake said nothing. Rake stayed at home and tried to ride out the storm. A lot of people, including many of those who played for him, thought, 'Well, Rake's finally killed a boy.' But a lot of the diehards were saying, 'Hell, that kid wasn't tough enough to be a Spartan.' The town split. It got ugly."

"I like this Reardon fellow," Neely said.

"He's tough. Late Monday night, he called Rake and fired him. Everything blew up Tuesday. Rake, typically, couldn't stand the thought of losing in any way, so he worked the phones, stirred up the boosters."

"No remorse?"

"Who knows how he felt? The funeral was a nightmare, as you might guess. All those kids bawling, some fainting. The players wearing green game jerseys. The band playing right along here at the graveside ceremony. Everybody was watching Rake, who looked quite pitiful."

"Rake was a great actor."

"And everybody knew it. He'd been fired

less than twenty-four hours earlier, so the funeral had the added drama of his departure. Quite a show, and nobody missed it."

"Wish I'd been here."

"Where were you?"

"Summer of '92? Out West somewhere. Probably Vancouver."

"The boosters tried to convene a massive meeting on Wednesday in the school gym. Reardon said, 'Not on this campus.' So they went to the VFW and had an Eddie Rake revival. Some of the hotheads threatened to cut off the money, boycott the games, picket Reardon's office, even start a new school, where I guess they would worship Rake."

"Was Rake there?"

"Oh no. He sent Rabbit. He was content to stay at home and work the phones. He truly believed that he could exert enough pressure to get his job back. But Reardon wasn't budging. He went to the assistants and named Snake Thomas as the new head coach. Snake declined. Reardon fired him. Donnie Malone said no. Reardon fired him. Quick Upchurch said no. Reardon fired him."

"I like this guy more and more."

"Finally, the Griffin brothers said they would fill in until someone was found. They played for Rake in the late seventies—"

"I remember them. The pecan orchard."

"That's them. Great players, nice guys, and because Rake never changed anything they knew the system, the plays, most of the kids. Friday night rolled around, first game of the season. We were playing Porterville, and the boycott was on. Problem was, nobody wanted to miss the game. Rake's folks, who were probably in the majority, couldn't stay away because they wanted the team to get slaughtered. The real fans were there for the right reasons. The place was packed, as always, with complicated loyalties yelling in all directions. The players were pumped. They dedicated the game to Scotty, and won by four touchdowns. A wonderful night. Sad, because of Scotty, and sad because the Rake era was apparently over, but winning is everything."

"This bench is hard," Neely said, standing. "Let's walk."

"Meanwhile, Rake hired a lawyer. A suit was filed, things got ugly, Reardon held his ground, and the town, though deeply divided, still managed to come together every Friday night. The team played with more guts than I've ever seen. Years later, one kid I know said it was such a relief playing football for the sheer fun of it, and not playing out of fear."

"How beautiful is that?"

"We never knew."

"No, we didn't."

"They won the first eight games. Undefeated. Nothing but pride and guts. There was talk of a state title. There was talk of a new streak. There was talk of paying the Griffins a bunch of money to start a new dynasty. All that crap."

"Then they lost?"

"Of course. It's football. A bunch of kids start thinking they're good, and they get their butts kicked."

"Who did it?"

"Hermantown."

"No, not Hermantown! That's a basketball school."

"Did it right here, in front of ten thousand. Worst game I ever saw. No pride, no guts, just show them the next press clipping. Forget a streak. Forget a state title. Fire the Griffins. Bring back Eddie Rake. Things were sort of okay when we were winning, but that one loss ripped this town apart for years. And when we lost the next week we failed to qualify for the playoffs. The Griffins quit immediately."

"Smart boys."

"Those of us who played for Rake were caught in the middle. Everyone asked, 'Which side are you on?' No fence straddling, bud, you had to declare if you were for Rake or against him."

"And you?"

"I straddled the fence and got kicked on both sides. It turned into class warfare. There had always been a very small group of people who were opposed to spending more money on football than on science and math combined. We traveled by chartered bus while every academic club carpooled with their parents. For years the girls had no softball field, while we had not one but two practice fields. The Latin Club qualified for a trip to New York but couldn't afford it; the same year the football team took the train to watch the Super Bowl in New Orleans. The list is endless.

Rake's firing made these complaints louder. The folks who wanted to deemphasize sports saw their opportunity. The football bubbas resisted; they just wanted Rake and another streak. Those of us who played, then went to college and were considered somewhat enlightened, got caught in the middle."

"What happened?"

"It smoldered and festered for months. John Reardon stood firm. He found some lost soul from Oklahoma who wanted to coach, and hired him as the successor to Eddie Rake. Unfortunately, '93 was reelection year for Reardon, so the whole mess turned into one huge political brawl. There was a strong rumor that Rake himself would run against Reardon. If he got elected, he would anoint himself Coach again and tell the whole world to go to hell. There was a rumor that Scotty's father would spend a million bucks to reelect John Reardon. And so on. The race was ugly before it started, so ugly that the Rake camp almost couldn't find a candidate."

"Who ran?"

"Dudley Bumpus."

"The name sounds promising."

"The name was the best part. He's a local real estate swinger who'd been a big mouth in the boosters. No political experience, no educational experience, barely finished college. Only one indictment, no conviction. A loser who almost won."

"Reardon held on?"

"By sixty votes. The turnout was the largest in the county's history, almost ninety percent. It was a war with no prisoners. When the winner was announced, Rake went home, locked the door, and hid for two years."

They stopped at a row of headstones. Paul walked along them, looking for someone. "Here," he said, pointing. "David Lee Goff. The first Spartan to die in Vietnam."

Neely looked at the headstone. There was an inlaid photograph of David Lee, looking all of sixteen years old, posing not in an Army uniform or a senior portrait, but in his green Spartan jersey, number 22. Born in 1950, killed in 1968. "I know his youngest brother," Paul was saying. "David Lee graduated in May, entered boot camp in June, arrived in Vietnam in October, died the day after Thanksgiving. Eighteen years and two months old."

"Two years before we were born."

"Something like that. There was another one who hasn't been found yet. A black kid, Marvin Rudd, who went missing in action in 1970."

"I remember Rake talking about Rudd," Neely said.

"Rake loved the kid. His parents still come to every game, and you wonder what they're thinking."

"I'm tired of death," Neely said. "Let's go."

Neely couldn't remember a bookshop in Messina, nor a place to get an espresso or buy coffee beans from Kenya. Nat's Place now provided all three, along with magazines, cigars, CDs, off-color greeting cards, herbal teas of dubious origin, vegetarian sandwiches and soups, and a meeting place for drifting poets and folksingers and the few wanna-be bohemians in the town. It was on the square, four doors down from Paul's bank, in a building that sold feed and fertilizer when

Neely was a kid. Paul had some loans to make, so Neely explored by himself.

Nat Sawyer was the worst punter in the history of Spartan football. His average yards per kick had set record lows, and he fumbled so many snaps that Rake would normally just go for it on fourth and eight, regardless of where the ball was. With Neely at quarterback, a good punter was not a necessity.

Twice, during their senior year, Nat had somehow managed to miss the ball with his foot entirely, creating some of the most watched video footage in the program's history. The second miss, which was actually two misses on the same punt, resulted in a comical ninety-four-yard touchdown run, which lasted, according to an accurate timing of the video, 17.3 seconds. Standing in his own end zone, and quite nervous about it, Nat had taken the snap, released the ball, kicked nothing but air, then been slaughtered by two defenders from Grove City. As the ball was spinning benignly on the ground nearby, Nat collected himself, picked it up, and began to run. The two defenders, who appeared to be stunned, gave a confused chase, and Nat tried an awkward punt-on-the-fly. When he missed, he picked up the ball again, and the race was on. The sight of such an ungainly gazelle lumbering down the field, in sheer terror, froze many of the players from both teams. Silo Mooney later testifed that he was laughing so hard he couldn't block for his punter. He swore he heard laughter coming from under the helmets of the Grove City players.

From the video, the coaches counted ten missed tackles. When Nat finally reached the end zone, he spiked the ball, didn't care about the penalty, ripped off his helmet, and rushed to the home side so the fans could admire him at close range.

Rake gave him an award for the Ugliest Touchdown of the Year.

In the tenth grade, Nat had tried playing safety, but he couldn't run and hated to hit. In the eleventh, he had tried receiver, but Neely nailed him in the gut on a slant and Nat couldn't breathe for five minutes. Few of Rake's players had been cursed with so little talent. None of Rake's players looked worse in a uniform.

The window was filled with books and advertised coffee and lunch. The door squeaked, a bell rattled, and for a moment Neely was stepping back in time. Then he got the first whiff of incense, and he knew Nat ran the place. The owner himself, hauling a stack of books, stepped from between two saggy shelves, and with a smile, said, "Good morning. Lookin' for something?"

Then he froze and the books fell to the floor. "Neely Crenshaw!" He lunged with as much awkwardness as he'd used punting a football, and the two embraced, a clumsy hug in which Neely caught a sharp elbow on his bicep. "It's great to see you!" Nat gushed, and for a second his eyes were wet.

"Good to see you, Nat," Neely said, slightly embarrassed. Fortunately, at that moment, there was only one other customer.

"You're looking at my earrings, aren't you?" Nat said, taking a step back.

"Well, yes, you have quite a collection." Each ear was loaded with at least five silver rings.

"First male earrings in Messina, how about that? And the first ponytail. And the first openly gay downtown merchant. Aren't you proud of me?" Nat was flipping his long black hair to show off his ponytail.

"Sure, Nat. You're looking good."

Nat was sizing him up, from head to toe, his eyes flashing as if he'd been guzzling espresso for hours. "How's your knee?" he asked, glancing around as if the injury was a secret.

"Gone for good, Nat."

"Sonofabitch hit you late. I saw it." Nat had the authority of someone standing on the sideline that day at Tech.

"A long time ago, Nat. In another life."

"How about some coffee? I got some stuff from Guatemala that gives one helluva buzz."

They wove through shelves and racks to the rear where an impromptu café materialized. Nat walked, almost ran, behind a cluttered counter and began slinging utensils. Neely straddled a stool and watched. Nothing Nat did was graceful.

"They say he's got less than twenty-four hours," Nat said, rinsing a small pot.

"Rumors are always reliable around here, especially about Rake."

"No, this came from someone inside the

house." The challenge in Messina was not to have the latest rumor, but to have the best source. "Wanna cigar? I got some smuggled Cubans. Another great buzz."

"No thanks. I don't smoke."

Nat was pouring water into a large, Italian-made machine. "What kinda work you doing?" he asked over his shoulder.

"Real estate."

"Man, that's original."

"Pays the bills. Pretty cool store you have here, Nat. Curry tells me you're doing well."

"I'm just trying to breathe some culture into this desert. Paul loaned me thirty thousand bucks to get started, can you believe that? I had nothing but an idea, and eight hundred bucks, and, of course, my mother was willing to sign the note."

"How's she doing?"

"Great, thanks. She refuses to age. Still teaching the third grade."

When the coffee was brewing properly, Nat leaned next to the small sink and stroked his bushy mustache. "Rake's gonna die, Neely, can you believe that? Messina without Eddie Rake.

He started coaching here forty-four years ago. Half the people in this county weren't born then."

"Have you seen him?"

"He was in here a lot, but when he got sick he went home to die. Nobody's seen Rake in six months."

Neely glanced around. "Rake was here?"

"Rake was my first customer. He encouraged me to open this place, gave me the standard pep talk—have no fear, work harder than the other guy, never say die—the usual halftime rah-rah. When I opened, he liked to sneak down here in the mornings for coffee. Guess he figured he was safe because there wasn't exactly a crowd. Most of the yokels thought they'd catch AIDS when they walked in the front door."

"When did you open?"

"Seven and a half years ago. Couldn't pay the light bill for the first two years, then it slowly came around. Rumor spread that this was Rake's favorite place, so the town got curious."

"I think the coffee's ready," Neely said as the machine hissed. "I never saw Rake read a book."

Nat poured two small cups, on saucers, and placed them on the counter.

"Smells potent," Neely said.

"It ought to require a prescription. Rake asked me one day what he might like to read. I gave him a Raymond Chandler. He came back the next day and asked for another. He loved the stuff. Then I gave him Dashiell Hammett. Then he went nuts over Elmore Leonard. I open at eight, one of the very few bookstores to do so, and once or twice a week Rake would come in early. We'd sit in the corner over there and talk about books; never football or politics, never gossip. Just books. He loved the detective stories. When we heard the bell ring on the front door, he would sneak out the back and go home."

"Why?"

Nat took a long sip of coffee, with the small cup disappearing into the depths of his unruly mustache. "We didn't talk about it much. Rake was embarrassed because he got sacked like that. He has enormous pride, something he taught us. But he also felt responsible for Scotty's death. A lot of people blamed him, and they always will. That's some serious baggage, man. You like the coffee?"

"Very strong. You miss him?"

Another slow sip. "How can you not miss Rake once you've played for him? I see his face every day. I hear his voice. I can smell him sweating. I can feel him hitting me, with no pads on. I can imitate his growl, his grumbling, his bitching. I remember his stories, his speeches, his lessons. I remember all forty plays and all thirty-eight games when I wore the jersey. My father died four years ago and I loved him dearly, but, and this is hard to say, he had less influence on me than Eddie Rake." Nat paused in mid-thought just long enough to pour more coffee. "Later, when I opened this place and got to know him as something other than a legend, when I wasn't worried about getting screamed at for screwing up, I grew to adore the old fart. Eddie Rake's not a sweet man, but he is human. He suffered greatly after Scotty's death, and he had no one to turn to. He prayed a lot, went to Mass every morning. I think fiction helped him; it was a new world. He got lost in books, hundreds of them, maybe thousands." A quick sip. "I miss him, sitting over there, talking about books and authors so he wouldn't have to talk about football."

The bell on the front door rattled softly in the distance. Nat shrugged it off and said, "They'll find us. You want a muffin or something?"

"No. I ate at Renfrow's. Everything's the same there. Same grease, same menu, same flies."

"Same bubbas sitting around bitchin' 'cause the team ain't undefeated."

"Yep. You go to the games?"

"Naw. When you're the only openly gay dude in a town like this, you don't enjoy crowds. People stare and point and whisper and grab their children, and, while I'm used to it, I'd rather avoid the scene. And I'd either go alone, which is no fun, or I'd take a date, which would stop the game. Can you imagine me walking in with some cute boy, holding hands? They'd stone us."

"How'd you manage to come out of the closet in this town?"

Nat put the coffee down and thrust his hands deep into the pockets of his highly starched and pressed jeans.

"Not here, man. After we graduated, I sort of migrated to D.C., where it didn't take me long to figure out who I am and what I am. I didn't sneak out of the closet, Neely, I kicked the damned door down. I got a job in a bookstore and learned the business. I lived the wild life for five years, had a ball, but then I got tired of the city. Frankly, I got homesick. My dad's health was declining, and I needed to come home. I had a long talk with Rake. I told him the truth. Eddie Rake was the first person here I confided in."

"What was his reaction?"

"He said he didn't know much about gay people, but if I knew who I was, then to hell with everybody else. 'Go live your life, son,' he said. 'Some folks'll hate you, some folks'll love you, most folks haven't made up their minds. It's up to you.' "

"Sounds like Rake."

"He gave me the courage, man. Then he convinced me to open this place, and when I was sure I had made a huge blunder, Rake started hanging around here and word spread. Just a second. Don't leave." Nat loped away toward the front where an elderly lady was waiting. He called her by name, in a voice that couldn't have been sweeter, and soon they were lost in a search for a book.

Neely walked around the counter and poured himself another cup of the brew. When Nat returned he said, "That was Mrs. Underwood, used to run the cleaners."

"I remember."

"A hundred ten years old and she likes erotic westerns. Go figure. You learn all sorts of good stuff when you run a bookshop. She figures she can buy from me because I have secrets of my own. Plus, at a hundred and ten, she probably doesn't give a damn anymore."

Nat put a massive blueberry muffin on a plate and laid it on the counter. "Dig in," he said, breaking it in half. Neely picked up a small piece.

"You bake this stuff?" Neely asked.

"Every morning. I buy it frozen, bake it in the oven. Nobody knows the difference."

"Not bad. You ever see Cameron?"

Nat stopped chewing and gave Neely a quizzical look. "Why should you be curious about Cameron?"

"You guys were friends. Just wondering."

"I hope your conscience still bothers you."

"It does."

"Good. I hope it's painful."

"Maybe. Sometimes."

"We write letters. She's fine, living in Chicago. Married, two little girls. Again, why do you ask?"

"I can't ask about one of our classmates?"

"There were almost two hundred in our class. Why is she the first you've asked about?"

"Please forgive me."

"No, I want to know. Come on, Neely, why ask about Cameron?"

Neely put a few crumbs of the muffin in his mouth and waited. He shrugged and smiled and said, "Okay, I think about her."

"Do you think about Screamer?"

"How could I forget?"

"You went with the bimbo, instant gratification, but in the long run it was a bad choice."

"I was young and stupid, I admit. Sure was fun, though."

"You were the all-American, Neely, you had your pick of any girl in the school. You dumped Cameron because Screamer was hot to trot. I hated you for it."

"Come on, Nat, really?"

"I hated your guts. Cameron was a close

friend from kindergarten, before you came to town. She knew I was different, and she always protected me. I tried to protect her, but she fell for you and that was a huge mistake. Screamer decided she wanted the all-American. The skirts got shorter, blouses tighter, and you were toast. My beloved Cameron got thrown aside."

"Sorry I brought this up."

"Yeah, man, let's talk about something else."

For a long, quiet moment there was nothing to talk about.

"Wait till you see her," Nat said.

"Pretty good, huh?"

"Screamer looks like an aging high-dollar call girl, which she probably is. Cameron is nothing but class."

"You think she'll be here?"

"Probably. Miss Lila taught her piano forever."

Neely had nowhere to go, but he glanced at his watch anyway. "Gotta run, Nat. Thanks for the coffee."

"Thanks for coming by, Neely. A real treat."

They zigzagged through the racks and shelves toward the front of the store. Neely stopped at the door. "Look, some of us are gathering in the bleachers tonight, sort of a vigil, I guess," he said. "Beer and war stories. Why don't you stop by?"

"I'd like that," Nat said. "Thanks."

Neely opened the door and started out. Nat grabbed his arm and said, "Neely, I lied. I never hated you."

"You should have."

"Nobody hated you, Neely. You were our all-American."

"Those days are over, Nat."

"No, not till Rake dies."

"Tell Cameron I'd like to see her. I have something to say."

———————

The secretary smiled efficiently and slid a clipboard across the counter. Neely printed his name, the time, and the date, and put down that he was visiting Bing Albritton, the longtime girls' basketball coach. The secretary examined the form, did not recognize either his face or his name, and finally said, "He's probably in the gym." The other lady in the administration office glanced up, and she too failed to recognize Neely Crenshaw.

And that was fine with him.

The halls of Messina High School were quiet, the classroom doors were all closed. Same lockers. Same paint color. Same floors hardened and shiny with layers of wax. Same sticky odor of disinfectant near the rest rooms. If he stepped into one he knew he would hear the same water dripping, smell the same smoke of a forbidden cigarette, see the same row of stained urinals, probably see the same fight between two punks. He kept to the hallways, where he passed Miss Arnett's algebra class, and with a quick glance through the narrow window in the door he caught a glimpse of his former teacher, certainly fifteen years older, sitting on the corner of the same desk, teaching the same formulas.

Had it really been fifteen years? For a moment he felt eighteen again, just a kid who hated algebra and hated English and needed nothing those classrooms had to offer because he would make his fortune on the football field. The rush and flurry of fifteen years passing made him dizzy for a second.

A janitor passed, an ancient gentleman who'd been cleaning the building since it was built. For a split second he seemed to recognize Neely, then he looked away and grunted a soft "Mornin'."

The main entrance of the school opened into a large, modern atrium that had been built when Neely was a sophomore. The atrium connected the two older buildings that comprised the high school and led to the entrance of the gymnasium. The walls were lined with senior class pictures, dating back to the 1920s.

Basketball was a second-level sport at Messina, but because of football the town had grown so accustomed to winning that it expected a dynasty from every team. In the late seventies, Rake had proclaimed that the school needed a new gym. A bond issue passed by ninety percent, and Messina had proudly built the finest high school basketball arena in the state. Its entrance was nothing but a hall of fame.

The centerpiece was a massive, and very expensive, trophy case in which Rake had carefully arranged his thirteen little monuments. Thirteen state titles, from 1961 to 1987. Behind each was a large team photo, with a list of the scores, and headlines blown up and mounted in a collage. There were signed footballs, and retired jerseys, including number 19. And there were lots of pictures of Rake—Rake with Johnny Unitas at some off-season function, Rake with a governor here and a governor there, Rake with Roman Armstead just after a Packers game.

For a few minutes, Neely was lost in the exhibit, though he'd seen it many times. It was at once a glorious tribute to a brilliant Coach and his dedicated players, and a sad reminder of what used to be. He once heard someone say that the lobby of the gym was the heart and soul of Messina. It was more of a shrine to Eddie Rake, an altar where his followers could worship.

Other display cases ran along the walls leading to the doors of the gym. More signed footballs, from less successful years. Smaller trophies, from less important teams. For the first time, and hopefully the last, Neely felt a twinge of regret for those Messina kids who had trained and succeeded and gone unnoticed because they played a lesser sport.

Football was king and that would never change. It brought the glory and paid the bills and that was that.

A loud bell, one that sounded so familiar, erupted nearby and jolted Neely back to the reality that he was trespassing fifteen years after his time. He headed back through the atrium, only to be engulfed in the fury and throng of a late-morning class change. The halls were alive with students pushing, yelling, slamming lockers, releasing the hormones and testosterone that had been suppressed for the past fifty minutes. No one recognized Neely.

A large, muscled player with a very thick neck almost bumped into him. He wore a green-and-white Spartan letterman's jacket, a status symbol with no equal in Messina. He had the customary strut of someone who owned the hall, which he did, if only briefly. He commanded respect. He expected to be admired. The girls smiled at him. The other boys gave him room.

"Come back in a few years, big boy, and they will not know your name," Neely thought. Your fabulous career will be a footnote. All the cute little girls will be mothers. The green jacket will still be a source of great personal pride, but you won't be able to wear it. High school stuff. Kids' stuff.

Why was it so important back then?

Neely suddenly felt very old. He ducked through the crowd and left the school.

———————

Late in the afternoon, he drove slowly along a narrow gravel road that wrapped around Karr's Hill. When the shoulder widened he pulled over and parked. Below him, an eighth of a mile away, was the Spartan field house, and in the distance to his right were the two practice fields where the varsity was hitting in full pads on one while the JV ran drills on the other. Coaches whistled and barked.

On Rake Field, Rabbit rode a green-and-yellow John Deere mower back and forth across the pristine grass, something he did every day from March until December. The cheerleaders were on the track behind the home bench painting signs for the war on Friday night and occasionally practicing some new maneuvers. In the far end zone, the band was assembling itself for a quick rehearsal.

Little had changed. Different coaches, different players, different cheerleaders, different kids in the band, but it was still the Spartans at Rake Field with Rabbit on the mower and everybody nervous about Friday. If Neely came back in ten years and witnessed the scene, he knew that the people and the place would look the same.

Another year, another team, another season.

It was hard to believe that Eddie Rake had been reduced to sitting very near where Neely was now sitting, and watching the game from so far away that he needed a radio to know what was happening. Did he cheer for the Spartans? Or did he secretly hope they lost every game, just for spite? Rake had a mean streak and could carry a grudge for years.

Neely had never lost here. His freshman team went undefeated, which was, of course, expected in Messina. The freshmen played on Thursday nights and drew more fans than most varsities. The two games he lost as a starter were both in the state finals, both on the campus at A&M. His eighth grade team had tied Porterville, at home, and that was as close as Neely had come to losing a football game in Messina.

The tie had prompted Coach Rake to charge into their dressing room and deliver a harsh postgame lecture on the meaning of Spartan pride. After he terrorized a bunch of thirteen-year-olds, he replaced their Coach.

The stories kept coming back as Neely watched the practice field. Having no desire to relive them, he left.

———

A man delivering a fruit basket to the Rake home heard the whispers, and before long the entire town knew that the Coach had drifted away so far that he would never return.

At dusk the gossip reached the bleachers, where small groups of players from different teams in different decades had gathered to wait. A few sat alone, deep in their own memories of Rake and glory that had vanished so long ago.

Paul Curry was back, in jeans and a sweatshirt and with two large pizzas Mona had made and sent so the boys could be boys for the night. Silo Mooney was there with a cooler of beer. Hubcap was missing, which was never a surprise. The Utley twins, Ronnie and Donnie, from out in the county had heard that Neely was back. Fifteen years earlier they had been identical 160-pound linebackers, each of whom could tackle an oak tree.

When it was dark, they watched as Rabbit made his trek to the scoreboard and flipped on the lights on the southwest pole. Rake was still alive, though barely. Long shadows fell across Rake Field, and the former players waited. The joggers were gone; the place was still. Laughter rose occasionally from one of the groups scattered throughout the home bleachers as someone told an old football story. But for the most part the voices were low. Rake was unconscious now, the end was near.

Nat Sawyer found them. He had something in a large carrying case. "You got drugs there, Nat?" Silo asked.

"Nope. Cigars."

Silo was the first to light up a Cuban, then Nat, then Paul, and finally Neely. The Utley twins neither drank nor smoked.

"You'll never guess what I found," Nat said.

"A girlfriend?" Silo said.

"Shut up, Silo." Nat opened the case and removed a large cassette tape player, a boom box.

"Great, some jazz, just what I wanted," Silo said.

Nat held up a cassette tape and announced, "This is Buck Coffey doing the '87 championship game."

"No way," Paul said.

"Yep. I listened to it last night, first time in years."

"I've never heard it," Paul said.

"I didn't know they recorded the games," Silo said.

"Lotta things you don't know, Silo," Nat said. He put the tape in the slot and began fiddling with the dials. "If it's okay with you guys, I thought we'd just skip the first half."

Even Neely managed a laugh. He'd thrown four interceptions and fumbled once in the first half. The Spartans were down 31–0 to a wonderfully gifted team from East Pike.

The tape began and the slow, raspy voice of Buck Coffey cut through the stillness of the bleachers.

*Buck Coffey here at halftime, folks, on the
campus of A&M, in what was supposed to be an
evenly matched game between two unbeaten
teams. Not so. East Pike leads in every category
except penalties and turnovers. The score is
thirty-one to nothing. I've been calling Messina
Spartan games for the past twenty-two years,
and I cannot remember being this far behind at
halftime.*

"Where's Buck now?" Neely asked.

"He quit when they sacked Rake," Paul
said.

Nat turned up the volume slightly and
Buck's voice carried even farther. It acted as a
magnet for the other players from the other
teams. Randy Jaeger and two of his teammates
from 1992 came over. Jon Couch the lawyer and
Blanchard Teague the optometrist were back in
their jogging shoes, with four others from the era
of The Streak. A dozen more moved close.

*The teams are back on the field, and we'll pause
for a word from our sponsors.*

"I cut out all that crap from the sponsors," Nat said.

"Good," said Paul.

"You're such a smart boy," Silo said.

I'm looking at the Messina sideline, and I don't see Coach Rake. In fact, none of the coaches are on the field. The teams are lining up for the second half kickoff, and the Spartan coaches are nowhere to be seen. This is very strange, to say the least.

"Where were the coaches?" someone asked.

Silo shrugged but didn't answer.

And that was the great question that had been asked and left unanswered for fifteen years in Messina. It had been obvious that the coaches boycotted the second half, but why?

East Pike is kicking to the south end zone. Here's the kick. It's short and taken by Marcus Mabry on the eighteen, zigs one way back the other, cuts upfield, has some room and is tackled at the thirty-yard line, where the Spartans will attempt to generate some offense for the first

*time tonight. Neely Crenshaw was just three for
fifteen in the first half. East Pike caught more of
his passes than the Spartans did.*

"Asshole," someone said.

"I thought he was on our side."

"Always, but he liked us better when we
were winning."

"Just wait," Nat said.

*Still no sign of Eddie Rake or the other coaches.
This is very bizarre. Spartans break huddle and
Crenshaw sets his offense. Curry wide right,
Mabry is the I-back. East Pike has eight men in
the box, just daring Crenshaw to throw the ball.
Here's the snap, option right, Crenshaw fakes
the pitch, cuts upfield, sees some daylight, hit
hard, spins, breaks a tackle, and he's loose at the
forty, the forty-five, the fifty, and out of bounds
at the East Pike forty-one, a pickup of twenty-
nine yards! The best play of the game for the
Spartan offense. Maybe they're coming to life.*

"Man, those guys hit," Silo said quietly.

"They had five Division One signees," Paul

said, reliving the nightmare of the first half. "Four on defense."

"You don't have to remind me," Neely said.

This Spartan team is finally awake. They're yelling at each other as they huddle, and the sideline is really fired up now. Here they come, Crenshaw points to his left and Curry spreads wide. Mabry in the slot, now in motion, the snap, quick pitch to Mabry, who scoots around left end for six, maybe seven yards. And the Spartans are really wired now. They're yanking each other off the turf, slapping each other on the helmets. And of course Silo Mooney is jawing with at least three of the East Pike players. Always a good sign.

"What were you saying, Silo?"

"I was telling them that they were about to get their asses kicked."

"You were down thirty-one points."

"Yep," Paul said. "It's true. We heard him. After that second play, Silo started the trash-talking."

*Second and three. Crenshaw in the shotgun. The
snap, a quick draw to Mabry, who hits hard,
spins, turns upfield to the thirty, the twenty,
and out of bounds at the East Pike sixteen!
Three plays, fifty-four yards! And the Spartan
offensive line is really moving people off the ball.
First down Spartans—in the first half they had
only five, and only forty-six yards rushing.
Crenshaw is calling his own plays now, nothing
from the sideline because there are no coaches
over there. Slot left with Curry wide, Mabry in
the I, Chenault in motion, option right, the fake,
the pitch to Mabry, who's hit at the line, runs
over the linebacker, and slams down to the ten-
yard line. Clock is ticking, ten-oh-five left in
the third quarter. Messina is ten yards from
a touchdown and a thousand miles from a
state title. First and goal, Crenshaw drops
back to pass, a draw to Mabry, who's hit in the
backfield, shakes loose, scoots wide to the
right. There's nobody there! He's gonna
score! He's gonna score! And Marcus Mabry
dives in for the first Messina touchdown!
Touchdown Spartans! The comeback has
begun!*

Jon Couch said, "When we scored, I remember thinking, 'Nice to have a touchdown, but there's no way we can come back on these guys.' East Pike was too good."

Nat turned the volume down and said, "They fumbled the kickoff, didn't they?"

Donnie: "Yep, Hindu stripped the ball on about the fifteen, we were swarming like hornets. It bounced around for about five minutes and finally rolled out of bounds at the twenty."

Ronnie: "They ran the tailback off-tackle right, no gain. Off-tackle left, no gain. Third and eleven, they dropped back to pass, Silo sacked the quarterback on the six-yard line."

Donnie: "Unfortunately, in doing so he stuffed him into the ground headfirst, fifteen yards, unsportsmanlike conduct, first down East Pike."

Silo: "It was a bad call."

Paul: "Bad call? You tried to break his neck."

Silo: "No, dear banker, I tried to kill him."

Ronnie: "We were out of our minds. Silo was growling like a wounded grizzly bear. Hindu, I swear, was crying. He wanted to blitz from safety on every play just so he could be sure he hit some-one."

Donnie: "We could have stopped the Dallas Cowboys."

Blanchard: "Who was calling the defense?"

Silo: "Me. It was simple—man coverage on the wideouts, knock down the tight end, eight guys in the box, everyone blitzed, everyone hit somebody, clean or not, didn't matter. It wasn't a game anymore, it was a war."

Donnie: "On third and eight, Higgins, that cocky flanker who went to Clemson, cut across the middle on a slant. The pass was high. Hindu read it perfectly, came across like a bullet train, and hit him a split second before the ball got there. Pass interference."

Paul: "His helmet went twenty feet in the air."

Couch: "We were forty rows up, and it sounded like two cars hitting."

Silo: "We celebrated. We'd killed one of 'em. Got a flag for that too."

Ronnie: "Two flags, thirty yards, we didn't care. They weren't going to score, didn't matter where they put the ball."

Blanchard: "You guys were convinced they couldn't score?"

Silo: "No team could've scored on us in that second half. When they finally carried Higgins off the field, on a stretcher I might add, the ball was on our thirty-yard line. They ran a sweep that lost six yards, a draw that lost four, then their little quarterback went to the shotgun again and we just mauled him."

Nat: "Their punter dropped one on the three-yard line."

Silo: "Yeah, they had a good punter. We, of course, had you."

Nat turned up the volume:

Ninety-seven yards to go for the Spartans, just under eight minutes left in the third quarter, still no sign of Eddie Rake or any of the Spartan coaches. I watched Crenshaw when East Pike had the ball. He kept his right hand in a bucket of ice the entire time, and he kept his helmet on. Handoff left side to Mabry, who doesn't get much. Both defenses are simply sending everybody, which should set up the pass.

Silo: "Not from the three-yard line, dumb-ass."

Paul: "Coffey always wanted to coach."

Pitch right side, Mabry bobbles the ball, then cuts upfield, got some room wide, and he's out of bounds along the ten.

Couch: "Just curious, Neely, do you know what you called next?"

Neely: "Sure, option right. I read the option, faked to Chenault, faked the pitch to Hubcap, cut upfield for eleven yards. The offensive line was chopping people down."

First and ten Spartans, who break huddle and sprint to the line of scrimmage. This is a different team, folks.

Paul: "I don't know why Buck was on the radio. Nobody was listening. The entire town was at the game."

Randy: "No, you're wrong. Everybody was listening. In the second half we were trying to find out what happened to Coach Rake, so all the

Messina fans had their radios stuck to their heads."

Handoff to Chenault, who plows straight ahead for three or four. He basically just lowered his helmet and followed Silo Mooney, who is being double-teamed.

Silo: "Just two! I was insulted. The second guy was this little nasty-faced bastard, weighed about one-eighty or so, thought he was bad. Came in the game trash-talking. He'll leave the field in just a minute."

Pitch to Mabry, wide right again, and he's got some room, up to the thirty and out of bounds. An East Pike youngster is shaken up on the field.

Silo: "That's him."
Blanchard: "What'd you do?"
Silo: "The play swept right, away from us. I chop-blocked him, got him on the ground, then dropped a knee into his stomach. Squealed

like a pig. He lasted for three plays. Never came back."

Paul: "They could've flagged us for unnecessary roughness on every play, offense or defense."

Neely: "While they dragged him off the field, Chenault tells me that their left tackle is not moving too well. Got something wrong, a twisted ankle maybe, the guy's in pain but won't leave the game. So we ran at him five straight times, same play. Six, seven yards a pop with Marcus low to the ground, just looking for someone to run over. I'd hand the ball off and watch the carnage."

Silo: "Turn it up, Nat."

First and ten on the East Pike thirty-eight. The Spartans are moving the ball but they're sure eating up the clock. Not a single pass so far in the second half. Six minutes to go. Curry in motion left, the snap, option right, the pitch to Mabry, who swings outside to the thirty! The twenty-five! All the way down to the East Pike eighteen, and the Spartans are knocking at the door!

Neely: "After every play, Mabry sprinted back to the huddle and said, 'Gimme the ball, bro, just gimme the ball.' So we did."

Paul: "And after Neely called every play, Silo would say, 'You fumble it, and I'll break your neck.'"

Silo: "I wasn't kidding, either."

Blanchard: "Were you guys aware of the clock?"

Neely: "Yeah, but it didn't matter. We knew we would win."

Mabry has carried the ball twelve times already in the second half, for seventy-eight yards. Here's a quick snap, right side again, not much there. The Spartans are really hammering away at the left side of the East Pike defense. Mabry just follows Durston and Vatrano, and of course Silo Mooney is always around the pileup.

Silo: "I loved Buck Coffey."

Neely: "Didn't you date his youngest daughter?"

Silo: "I wouldn't call it dating. Buck damned sure didn't know anything about it."

Second and eight, from the sixteen, Mabry again
off the right side, for three, maybe four, and it's a
dogfight down there in the trenches, folks.

Silo: "It's always a dogfight, Buck, that's
why they call it the trenches."

In the semidarkness, the fraternity had quietly grown larger. Other players had eased over
or slid down the bleachers, close enough to hear
the play-by-play.

Third and four, Curry wide, full backfield,
option right, Crenshaw keeps, is hit, falls
forward for maybe two. He really got nailed by
Devon Bond.

Neely: "Devon Bond hit me so many times I
felt like a punching bag."

Silo: "He was the one player I couldn't do
anything with. I'd fire off the ball, have a perfect
shot at him, and he'd just vanish. That, or he'd hit
me a forearm that would rattle my teeth. He was
one bad dude."

Donnie: "Didn't he make a roster?"

John Grisham

Paul: "Steelers, for a couple of years, then some injuries sent him back to East Pike."

A fourth and two that is beyond huge, folks. Spartans must score here, because they have a lot more scoring to do. And the clock is really moving now. Three minutes and forty seconds. Full house, now Chenault in motion left, long count by Crenshaw. And they jump! East Pike jumps offside! First and goal Spartans on the five-yard line! Crenshaw gave it the old head fake and got by with it.

Silo: "Head fake my ass."

Paul: "It was all in the cadence."

Blanchard: "I remember their Coach going crazy, charging the field."

Neely: "He got a flag. Half the distance."

Silo: "That guy was psycho, and the more we scored the louder he screamed."

First and goal from the two and a half. Option left, here comes the pitch, Marcus Mabry is hit, drives, and falls into the end zone! Touchdown Spartans! Touchdown!

Buck's voice carried even farther through the still night. Rabbit, at some point, heard it and crept into the shadows down the track to investigate the noise. He saw a crowd sitting and half-lying haphazardly up in the bleachers. He saw bottles of beer, smelled the smoke from the cigars. In another era, he would have taken charge and ordered everyone away from the field. But those were Rake's boys up there, the chosen few. They were waiting for the lights to go off.

If he got closer he could call each one by name, and number, and he could remember the exact location of their lockers.

Rabbit slipped through the metal braces under the bleachers and hid below the players, listening.

Silo: "Neely called for an onside kick, and it almost worked. The ball bounced around and got touched by every damned player on the field until some guy with the wrong jersey finally found a handle."

Ronnie: "They ran twice for two yards, then tried a long pass that Hindu broke up. Three and out, except that Hindu leveled the receiver out of bounds. Unnecessary roughness. First down."

Donnie: "It was a horrible call."

Blanchard: "We went crazy in the stands."

Randy: "My father almost threw his radio on the field."

Silo: "We didn't care. They weren't going to score."

Ronnie: "They went three and out again."

Couch: "Wasn't the punt return somewhere around here?"

Nat: "First play of the fourth quarter."

He turned up the volume.

East Pike back to punt on the Messina forty-one, the snap, a low, hard kick, taken on the bounce by Paul Curry at the five, wide to the right to the ten, cuts back— He's got a wall! A perfect wall! To the twenty, thirty, forty! Cuts back across midfield, picks up a block from Marcus Mabry, to the forty, the thirty, along the far sideline! He's got blockers everywhere! To the ten, five, four, two, touchdown!! Touchdown Spartans! A ninety-five-yard punt return!

Nat turned the volume down so they could savor one of the greatest moments in Spartan football history. The punt return had been executed with textbook precision, every block and every move choreographed by Eddie Rake during endless hours of practice. When Paul Curry danced into the end zone he was escorted by six green jerseys, just the way they'd been drilled. "We all meet in the end zone," Rake had screamed, over and over.

Two East Pike players were down, victims of vicious, but legal, blindside blocks that Rake had taught them in the ninth grade. "Punt returns are perfect for killing people," he'd said, over and over.

Paul: "Let's listen to it again."

Silo: "Once is enough. Same ending."

After the field was cleared, East Pike took the following kickoff and began a drive that would consume six minutes. For one brief period in the second half, they used their superior talent to chew up sixty yards, though every inch was contested. Their seamless execution of the first half was long gone, replaced by stutter steps and uncertainty. The sky was falling. One massive choke was under way, and they were powerless to stop it.

John Grisham

Every handoff drew a furious attack from all eleven defenders. Every short pass ended with the receiver crumpled on the ground. There was no time for long passes; Silo could not be contained. On fourth and two from the Messina twenty-eight, East Pike foolishly went for the first down. The quarterback faked a pitch to the left, bootlegged to the right, looking for the tight end. The tight end, however, had been mauled at the line by Donnie Utley, whose twin was blitzing like a mad dog. Ronnie caught the quarterback from behind, stripped the ball like he'd been taught, flung him to the ground, and the Spartans, trailing 31–21, were in business with five thirty-five to go in the game.

There's something wrong with Neely's right hand, not a single pass attempt in the second half. When the defense is on the field he keeps it buried in an ice bucket. East Pike has it figured out— they're in man coverage on the wideouts, everybody else is packed along the line of scrimmage.

Jaeger: "It was broken, wasn't it?"
Paul: "Yes, it was broken."

Neely just nodded.

Jaeger: "How'd you break it, Neely?"

Silo: "A locker-room incident."

Neely was silent.

First and ten from the Spartan thirty-nine,
Curry wide right, motion left, pitch right side to
Marcus Mabry, who gets four, maybe five very
tough yards. Devon Bond is all over the field.
Must be a linebacker's dream, not worrying
about pass coverage, just stalking the football.
Spartans huddle quickly, sprint to the line, they
can hear the clock. Quick snap, dive to
Chenault, right behind Silo Mooney, who is just
slaughtering people in the middle of field.

Silo: "I like that—slaughtering."

Donnie: "That was putting it mildly. Frank missed a block on a sweep, and Silo punched him in the huddle."

Neely: "He didn't punch him. He slapped him. The referee started to throw a flag, but he wasn't sure if you could be penalized for roughing up your own teammates."

Silo: "He shouldn't have missed the block."

*Third and one at the forty-eight, four-twenty to
go in the game, Spartans are back at the line
before East Pike is set, quick snap, Neely rolling
right, a keeper, across the fifty to the forty-five
and out of bounds. First down and the clock will
stop. The Spartans need two touchdowns.
They'll have to start using the sidelines.*

Silo: "Go for it, Buck, why don't you just call
the plays?"

Donnie: "I'm sure he knew them."

Randy: "Hell, everybody knew them. They
didn't change in over thirty years."

Couch: "We ran the same plays you guys
were running against East Pike."

*Mabry off tackle again, for four yards, hit hard
by Devon Bond and the safety, Armondo Butler,
a real headhunter. They have no fear of the pass,
so they're really loading up against the run.
Double tight end set, Chenault in motion right,
option left, pitch to Mabry, who spins forward,
keeps chugging, somehow picks up three. It'll be
third and three now, another big play, but
they're all big now. Clock's counting, under four*

*minutes to play. Ball at the thirty-eight. Curry
sprints from the huddle, wide left, split
backfield, Neely drops back into the shotgun,
the snap, he rolls right, looking, looking, there's
pressure, and off he goes to the far side, and
he's nailed by Devon Bond. A really nasty
helmet to helmet collision, and Neely is slow
getting up.*

Neely: "I couldn't see. I've never been hit
that hard, and for thirty seconds or so I couldn't
see."

Paul: "We didn't want to waste a time-out,
so we yanked him up, got him to his feet, sorta
dragged him back to the huddle."

Silo: "I slapped him too, and that really
helped."

Neely: "I don't remember that."

Paul: "It was fourth and one. Neely was in
la-la land, so I called the play. What can I say, I'm
a genius."

*Fourth and one, Spartans are slow coming to the
line. Crenshaw doesn't feel too well right now,
doesn't look too steady. Huge play. Huge play.*

This could be the ballgame, folks. East Pike has nine men on the line. Double tight ends, no wideouts. Crenshaw finds the center, long snap, quick pitch to Mabry, who stops, jumps, shovels a pass across the middle to Heath Dorcek, who's wide open! To the thirty! The twenty! Hit at the ten! Stumbles and falls down to the three! First and goal Spartans!

Paul: "It was the ugliest pass ever thrown in organized football. End over end, a dying duck. Man, was it beautiful."

Silo: "Gorgeous. Dorcek couldn't catch the flu; that's why Neely never threw to him."

Nat: "I've never seen anyone run so slow, just a big lumbering buffalo."

Silo: "He could outrun your ass."

Neely: "The play took forever, and when Heath came back to the huddle he had tears in his eyes."

Paul: "I looked at Neely, and he said, 'Call a play.' I remember looking at the clock—three forty to go, and we had to score twice. I said, 'Let's do it now, not on third down.' Silo said, 'Run it up my back.'"

Only three yards from the promised land, folks,
and here come the Spartans, hustling to the line,
quick set, quick snap, Crenshaw on a keeper, and
he walks into the end zone! Silo Mooney and
Barry Vatrano bulldozed the entire center of the
East Pike line! Touchdown Spartans!
Touchdown Spartans! They will not be denied!
Thirty-one to twenty-seven! Unbelievable!

Blanchard: "I remember you guys huddled together before you kicked off, the entire team. Almost got a delay of game."

There was a long pause. Finally Silo spoke.

Silo: "We were taking care of business. Had some secrets to protect."

Couch: "Secrets about Rake?"

Silo: "Yep."

Couch: "Doesn't he show up about now?"

Paul: "We weren't watching, but at some point after we kicked off, word spread down the sideline that Rake was back. We spotted him at the edge of the end zone, just standing there with the other four coaches, still wearing their green sweatshirts, hands in pockets, watching nonchalantly as if they were the grounds crew or something. We hated the sight of them."

Nat: "It was us versus them. We didn't care about East Pike."

Blanchard: "I'll never forget that sight—Rake and his assistants at the edge of the field, looking like a bunch of whores in church. At the time we didn't know why they were over there. Still don't, I guess."

Paul: "They were told to stay away from our sideline."

Blanchard: "By whom?"

Paul: "The team."

Blanchard: "But why?"

Nat reached for the volume. Buck Coffey's voice was beginning to crack as the excitement took its toll. To compensate for the fading strength and clarity, Buck was just getting louder. When East Pike walked to the line on first down, Buck was practically yelling into his microphone.

Ball on the eighteen, clock still at three twenty-five to go. East Pike has a grand total of three first downs and sixty-one yards of offense in the second half. Everything they've tried has been stuffed down their throats by an inspired bunch of Spartans. A magnificent turnaround, the gutsiest performance I've seen in twenty-two years of calling Spartan football.

Silo: "Go for it, Buck."

Handoff right side, for one, maybe two yards. East Pike is not sure what to do right now. They'd love to burn some clock, but they need to get some first downs. Three minutes, ten seconds, and the clock is running. Messina with all three time-outs left, and they're gonna need them. East Pike really dragging now, slow to the huddle, slow with the play from the sidelines, play clock down to twelve, they break huddle, slow to the line. Four, three, two, one, the snap, pitch right to Barnaby, who scoots around the corner for five, maybe six. A big third down now, third and three on the twenty-five, with the clock moving.

A car rolled to a stop near the gate. It was white with words painted on the doors. "I guess Mal's back," someone said. The Sheriff took his time getting out, stretched, surveyed the field and the stands. Then he lit a cigarette, the flicker of the lighter visible thirty rows up, on the forty-yard line.

Silo: "Shoulda brought more beer."

Spartans dig in. Wideouts right and left. In the shotgun, Waddell takes the snap, fakes right, then throws left, ball is caught at the thirty-two on quick slant by Gaddy, who is slammed down to the ground by Hindu Aiken. First down East Pike, and they're moving the chains. Two forty to go, and the Spartans need somebody on the sideline to start making some decisions. They're playing without coaches down there, folks.

Blanchard: "Who was making decisions?"

Paul: "After they got the first down, Neely and I decided we'd better burn a time-out."

Silo: "I took the defense to the sideline and the whole team gathered around. Everyone was screaming. I get goose bumps thinking about it now."

Neely: "Volume, Nat, before Silo starts crying."

First down at the thirty-two. East Pike breaks
huddle, in no hurry, split backfield, wide right,
the snap, Waddell back to pass, looking right,
and he connects on a down-and-out at the
thirty-eight. The receiver did not go out of
bounds, and the clock is moving at two twenty-
eight. Two twenty-seven.

From the gate, Mal Brown smoked his
cigarette and studied the crowd of ex-Spartans
sprawled loosely together in the center of the
bleachers. He could hear the radio and he recognized Buck Coffey's voice, but he could not tell
what game they were listening to. He had a
hunch, though. He puffed and looked for Rabbit
somewhere in the shadows.

East Pike at the line with a second and four, two
minutes fourteen seconds to go in the game.
Quick pitch left to Barnaby, and he cannot go!
Hit hard at the line by both Utleys, Ronnie and
Donnie blitzing through every gap, it seems.
They hit him first and the entire team piled on!
The Spartans are in a frenzy down there, but

they'd better be careful. There was almost a
late hit.

Silo: "Late hit, unnecessary roughness, half a
dozen personal fouls, take your pick Buck. They
could've flagged us on every play."

Ronnie: "Silo was biting people."

Third and four, under two minutes. East Pike
stalling as much as they can as the clock ticks
away. Back at the line all eleven Spartans are
waiting. Do you run and get stuffed, or do you
pass and get sacked?That's the choice for East
Pike. They cannot move the ball! Waddell is
back, it's a screen, and the ball is knocked down
by Donnie Utley! Clock stops! Fourth and
four! East Pike will have to punt! One minute
fifty seconds to play and the Spartans will get
the ball!

Mal was walking slowly around the track,
with another cigarette. They watched him get
nearer.

Paul: "The last punt return worked, so we
decided to try it again."

*A low punt, a line drive that hits on the forty,
takes a big bounce and then another, Alonzo
Taylor scoops it at the thirty-five and he has
nowhere to go! Flags everywhere! Could be a
clip!*

Paul: "Could be? Hindu drilled a guy dead
in the back, the worst clip I've ever seen."

Silo: "I started to break his neck."

Neely: "I stopped you, remember? Poor guy
came to the sideline crying."

Silo: "Poor guy. If I saw him now I'd remind
him of that clip."

*And so it comes down to this, folks. The
Spartans have the ball on their own nineteen,
eighty-one yards to go, with one minute and
forty seconds left on the clock. Down thirty-one
to twenty-eight. Crenshaw has two time-outs
and no passing game.*

Paul: "Couldn't pass with a broken hand."

*The entire Spartan team is huddled together on
the sideline and it looks like they're having a
prayer.*

Mal was walking up the steps, slowly, with none of his customary purpose and banter. Nat stopped the tape, and the bleachers were still.

"Boys," Mal said softly, "Coach is gone."

Rabbit materialized from the shadows and loped down the track. They watched as he disappeared behind the scoreboard, and a few seconds later the bank of lights on the southwest pole went off.

Rake Field was dark.

———

Most of the Spartans sitting quietly in the bleachers did not know Messina without Eddie Rake. And for the older ones who were very young when he arrived as an unknown and untested twenty-eight-year-old football coach, his influence on the town was so overpowering that it was easy to assume he'd always been there. After all, Messina as a town didn't matter before Rake. It wasn't on the map.

The vigil was over. The lights were off.

Though they had been waiting for his impending death, Mal's message hit them hard. Each of the Spartans withdrew to his own memories for a few moments. Silo set his beer bottle down and began tapping both temples with his fingers. Paul Curry rested his elbows on his knees and stared at the field, at a spot somewhere around the fifty-yard line where his Coach would storm and fuss, and when a game was tight no one would get near him. Neely could see Rake in the hospital room, green Messina cap in hand, talking softly to his ex–all-American, concerned about his knee and his future. And trying to apologize.

Nat Sawyer bit his lip as his eyes began to moisten. Eddie Rake meant much more to him after his football days. "Thank God it was dark," Nat thought to himself. But he knew there were other tears.

Somewhere across the little valley, from the direction of the town, came the soft chimes of church bells. Messina was getting the news that it dreaded most.

Blanchard Teague spoke first. "I really want to finish this game. We've been waiting for fifteen years."

Paul: "We ran flood-right, Alonzo got about six or seven, and made it out of bounds."

Silo: "Woulda scored but Vatrano missed a block on a linebacker. I told him I'd castrate him in the locker room if he missed another one."

Paul: "They had everybody at the line. I kept asking Neely if he could throw anything, even a little jump pass over the middle, anything to loosen up their secondary."

Neely: "I could barely grip the ball."

Paul: "Second down, we swept left—"

Neely: "No, second down, we sent three wide and deep, I dropped back to pass, then tucked it and ran, got sixteen yards but couldn't get out of bounds. Devon Bond hit me again and I thought I was dead."

Couch: "I remember that. But he was slow getting up too."

Neely: "I wasn't worried about him."

Paul: "Ball was on the forty, about a minute to go. Didn't we sweep again?"

Nat: "To the left, almost a first down, and Alonzo got out of bounds, right in front of our bench."

Neely: "Then we tried the option pass again, and Alonzo threw it away, almost got it picked off."

Nat: "It was picked off, but the safety had one foot over the line."

Silo: "That's when I told you no more passes from Alonzo."

Couch: "What was it like in the huddle?"

Silo: "Pretty tense, but when Neely said shut up, we shut up. He kept tellin' us we were stickin' it down their throats, that we were gonna win, and, as always, we believed him."

Nat: "The ball was on the fifty with fifty seconds to go."

Neely: "I called a screen pass, and it worked beautifully. The pass rush was ferocious, and I managed to shovel the ball to Alonzo with my left hand."

Nat: "It was beautiful. He got hit in the backfield, broke away, and suddenly he had a wall of blockers."

Silo: "That's when I got Bond, caught that sumbitch fightin' off one block and not lookin,' buried my helmet in his left side and they carried him off."

Neely: "That probably won the game."

Blanchard: "The place was a madhouse,

thirty-five thousand people screaming like idiots, but we still heard the hit you put on Bond."

Silo: "It was legal. I preferred the ones that were not legal, but it was a bad time for a penalty."

Paul: "Alonzo picked up about twenty. The clock stopped with the injury, so we had some time. Neely called three plays."

Neely: "I didn't want to risk an interception or a fumble, and the only way to spread the defense was to send the receivers wide and go from the shotgun. On first down I scrambled for about ten."

Nat: "Eleven. It was first down at the twenty-one with thirty seconds to go."

Neely: "With Bond out of the game, I knew I could score. I figured two more scrambles and we'd be in the end zone. In the huddle, I told them to make sure they put somebody on the ground."

Silo: "I told 'em to kill somebody."

Neely: "They blitzed all three linebackers and I got nailed at the line. We had to burn our last time-out."

Amos: "Did you think about a field goal?"

Neely: "Yeah, but Scobie had a weak leg—accurate but weak."

Paul: "Plus, he hadn't kicked a field goal all year."

Silo: "The kicking game was not our strongest suit."

Nat: "Thanks, Silo. I can always count on you."

The final play of the miracle drive was perhaps the most famous in all of the glorious history of Spartan football. With no time-outs, twenty yards to go, eighteen seconds left, Neely sent two receivers wide, and took the snap in the shotgun. He quickly handed off to Marcus Mabry on a draw. Marcus took three steps, then abruptly stopped and pitched the ball back to Neely, who sprinted to his right, pumping the ball as if he would finally throw it. When he turned upfield, the offensive line released and sprinted forward, looking for someone to level. At the ten, Neely, running like a madman, lowered his head and crashed into a linebacker and a safety, a collision that would have knocked out a mere mortal. He spun away, free but dizzy, legs still churning, got hit again at the five, and again at the three where most of the East Pike defense managed to corral him. The play was almost over, as was the game, when Silo Mooney and Barry Vatrano slammed into the mass of humanity hanging on Neely, and the entire pile fell into the end zone. Neely sprang to his feet, still clutching the ball, and looked directly at Eddie Rake, twenty feet away, motionless and noncommittal.

Neely: "For a split second, I thought about spiking the ball at him, but then Silo flung me down and everybody jumped on."

Nat: "The whole team was down there. Along with the cheerleaders, the trainers, and half the band. Got fifteen yards for excessive celebrating."

Couch: "Nobody cared. I remember looking at Rake and the coaches, and they didn't move. Talk about weird."

Neely: "I was lying in the end zone, getting crushed by my teammates, telling myself that we'd just done the impossible."

Randy: "I was twelve years old, and I remember all the Messina fans were just sitting there, stunned, exhausted, a lot of them crying."

Blanchard: "The folks from East Pike were crying too."

Randy: "They ran one play, didn't they? After the kickoff?"

Paul: "Yeah, Donnie blitzed and nailed the quarterback. The game was over."

Randy: "All of a sudden, every player with a green jersey was sprinting off the field—no hand-shakes, no postgame huddle, just a mad rush to get to the locker room. The entire team vanished."

Mal: "We thought y'all'd gone crazy. We waited for a spell, thinkin' you had to come back to get the trophy and all."

Paul: "We weren't coming out. They sent someone to retrieve us for the ceremony, but we kept the door locked."

Couch: "Those poor kids from East Pike tried to smile when they got the runner-up tro-phy, but they were still in shock."

Blanchard: "Rake had vanished too. Some-how they got Rabbit to walk out to midfield and accept the championship trophy. It was very strange, but we were too excited to care."

Mal walked up to Silo's cooler and pulled

out a beer. "Help yourself there, Sheriff," Silo said.

"I'm off duty." He took a long sip and began walking down the steps. "Funeral's Friday, boys. At noon."

"Where?"

"Here. Where else?"

Thursday

Neely and Paul met early Thursday morning in the rear of the bookstore, where Nat brewed another pot of his highly addictive and probably illegal Guatemalan coffee. Nat had business up front, near the tiny and semi-hidden occult section, with a sinister-looking woman who had pale skin and jet-black hair. "The town witch," Paul said somewhat proudly, as if every town needed a witch, and very softly, as if she might fling a curse their way.

The Sheriff arrived a few minutes after eight, fully uniformed and heavily armed and looking quite lost in the only bookstore in the county, and one owned by a homosexual at that. Had Nat not been a former Spartan, Mal would've probably had him under surveillance as a suspicious character.

"You boys ready?" he growled, obviously anxious to leave.

With Neely in the front seat and Paul in the back, they sped away from downtown in a long white Ford with bold lettering along the doors, announcing that the car was the property of the SHERIFF. On the main highway, Mal pushed the accelerator and flipped a switch turning on the flashing red and blue lights. No sirens, though. Once everything was properly configured, he cocked his weight to one side, picked up his tall Styrofoam cup of coffee, and laid a limp wrist over the top of the wheel. They were doing a hundred miles an hour.

"I was in Vietnam," Mal announced, selecting the topic and giving the impression that he might talk nonstop for the next two hours. Paul sank a few inches in the rear seat, like a real criminal on the way to a court hearing. Neely watched the traffic, certain they were about to be slaughtered in some gruesome two-lane pileup.

"I was on a PBR on the Bassac River." A loud slurp of coffee as the setting was established. "There were six of us on this stupid little boat about twice the size of a nice bass rig, and our job was to patrol up and down the river and make trouble. Anythang that moved, we shot it. We were idiots. A cow gets too close, target practice. A nosy rice farmer raises his head up from the rice paddy, we'd start firin' just to watch him hit the mud. Our mission each day had no tactical purpose whatsoever, so we drank beer, smoked pot, played cards, tried to entice the local girls to go boatin' with us."

"I'm sure this is going somewhere," Paul said from the rear.

"Shut up and listen. One day we're half asleep, it's hot, we're sunbathin', nappin' like a bunch of turtles on a log, when, suddenly, all hell breaks loose. We're takin' fire from both sides of the river. Heavy fire. An ambush. Two guys were below. I'm on the deck with three others, all of whom get hit immediately. Dead. Shot before they could get their guns. Blood flyin' through the air. Everybody screamin'. I'm flat on my stomach, unable to move, when a fuel barrel gets hit. Damned thing wasn't supposed to be on deck, but what did we care? We were invincible because we were eighteen and stupid. The thing explodes. I manage to dive into the river without gettin' burned. I swim up beside the boat and grab a piece of camouflage nettin' that's hangin' over the side. I hear my two buddies screamin' inside the boat. They're trapped, smoke and fire everywhere, no way out. I stay underwater as long as I can. Whenever I pop up for air, the gooks spray gunfire all around me. Heavy gunfire. They know I'm in the water holdin' my breath. This goes on for a long time while the boat burns and drifts with the current. The screamin' and coughin' finally stops down in the cabin, ever'body's dead but me. The gooks are out in the open now, walkin' along the banks on both sides, out for a Sunday stroll. All fun and games. I'm the last guy alive, and they're waitin' for me to make a mistake. I swim under the boat, pop up on the other side, take some air, bullets everywhere. I swim to the rear, grab the rudder for a while, come up for air, hear the gooks laughin' as they spray me. The river is full of snakes, these short little bastards that are deadly poisonous. So I figure I got three choices—drown, get shot, or wait for the snakes."

Mal placed the coffee in a holder on the dash and lit a cigarette. Mercifully, he cracked his window. Neely cracked his as well. They were in farmland, speeding through rolling hills, flying past farm tractors and old pickups.

"So what happened?" Neely asked when it became apparent that Mal wanted prompting.

"You know what saved me?"

"Tell us."

"Rake. Eddie Rake. When I was hangin' on for my life, under that boat, I didn't think about my momma or my dad or my girlfriend, I thought about Rake. I could hear him barkin' at us at the end of practice when we were runnin' sprints. I remembered his locker-room speeches. Never quit, never quit. You win because you're tougher mentally than the other guy, and you're tougher mentally because your trainin' is superior. If you're winnin', never quit. If you're losin', never quit. If you're hurt, never quit."

A long pull on the cigarette while the two

younger men digested the story. Meanwhile, outside the car, civilian drivers swerved onto shoulders and hit brakes to make way for this law enforcement emergency.

"I finally got hit, in the leg. Did you know bullets can get you underwater?"

"Never really thought about it," Neely admitted.

"Damned right they can. Left hamstring. I never felt such pain, like a hot knife. I almost passed out from the pain, and I was gaspin' for breath. Rake expected us to play hurt, so I told myself Rake was watchin'. Rake was up there somewhere, on the side of the river, watchin' to see how tough I was."

A long cancerous draw on the cigarette; a halfhearted effort to blow the smoke out the window. A long pause as Mal was lost in the horror of this memory. A minute passed.

"Obviously you survived," Paul said, anxious to get to the end of it.

"I was lucky. The other five got boxed up and shipped home. The boat burned and burned and at times I couldn't hang on because the hull was so hot. Then the batteries exploded, sounded like direct mortar hits, and she started to sink. I could hear the gooks laughin'. I could also hear Rake in the fourth quarter, 'Time to suck it up and go, men. Here's where we win or lose. Gut check, gut check.'"

"I can hear him too," Neely said.

"All of a sudden, the shootin' stopped. Then I heard choppers. Two of them had seen the smoke and decided to explore. They came in low, scattered the gooks, dropped a rope, and I got out. When they hauled me in I looked down and saw the boat burnin.' I saw two of my buddies lying on the deck, burnt black. I was in shock and finally passed out. They told me later that when they asked me my name, I said, 'Eddie Rake.'"

Neely glanced to his left as Mal turned away. His voice cracked just a little, then he wiped his eyes. No hands on the wheel for a couple of seconds.

"So you came home?" Paul said.

"Yeah, that was the lucky part. I got outta there. You boys hungry?"

"No."

"No."

Evidently Mal was. He stomped the brake

pedal while veering to the right, onto a gravel lot in front of an old country store. The Ford fish-tailed as Mal brought it to a violent stop. "Best damned biscuits in this part of the state," he said as he yanked open his door and stepped out into a cloud of dust. They followed him to the rear, through a rickety screen door, and into some-one's small and smoky kitchen. Four tables were packed close together, all surrounded by rustic-looking gentlemen devouring ham and biscuits. Fortunately, at least for Mal, who appeared to be ready to collapse from hunger, there were three empty stools at the cluttered counter. "Need some biscuits over here," he growled at a tiny old woman hovering over a stove. Evidently, menus were not needed.

With remarkable speed, she served them coffee and biscuits, with butter and sorghum molasses. Mal plunged into the first one, a thick brownish concoction of lard and flour that weighed at least a pound. Neely, on his left, and Paul, on his right, followed along.

"Heard you boys talkin' last night up in the bleachers," Mal said, shifting from Vietnam to football. He took a large bite and began chewing ferociously. "About the '87 game. I was there, so was everybody else. We figured somethin' happened at halftime, in the locker room, some kind of altercation between you and Rake. Never heard the real story, you know, 'cause you boys never talked about it."

"You could call it an altercation," Neely said, still prepping his first and only biscuit.

"No one's ever talked about it," Paul said.

"So what happened?"

"An altercation."

"Got that. Rake's dead now."

"So?"

"So, it's been fifteen years. I wanna know the story," Mal said as if he were drilling a murder suspect in the back room of the jail.

Neely put the biscuit on his plate and stared at it. Then he glanced over at Paul, who nodded. Go ahead. You can finally tell the story.

Neely sipped his coffee and ignored the food. He stared at the counter and drifted away. "We were down thirty-one to zip, just getting the hell beaten out of us," he said slowly and very softly.

"I was there," Mal said, chewing without interruption.

"We got to the locker room at halftime and waited for Rake. We waited and waited, knowing that we were about to be eaten alive. He finally walked in, with the other coaches. He was way beyond furious. We were terrified. He walked straight up to me, pure hatred in his eyes. I had no idea what to expect. He said, 'You miserable excuse for a football player.' I said, 'Thanks, Coach.' As soon as I got the words out, he took his left hand and backhanded me across the face."

"It sounded like a wooden bat hitting a baseball," Paul said. He, too, had lost interest in the food.

"That broke your nose?" Mal said, still quite interested in his breakfast.

"Yep."

"What'd you do?"

"By instinct, I swung. I didn't know if he planned to hit me again, and I wasn't about to wait. So I threw a right hook with everything I could put into it. Caught him perfectly on the left jaw, flush to the face."

"It wasn't a right hook," Paul said. "It was a

bomb. Rake's head jerked like he'd been shot, and he fell like a bag of cement."

"Knocked him out?"

"Cold. Coach Upchurch rushed forward, yelling, cussing, like he was going to finish me off," Neely said. "I couldn't see, there was blood all over my face."

"Silo stepped up and grabbed Upchurch by the throat with both hands," Paul said. "He lifted him up, threw him against the wall, said he'd kill him right there if he made another move. Rake was dead on the floor. Snake Thomas and Rabbit and one of the trainers were squatting beside him. It was chaos for a few seconds, then Silo threw Upchurch to the floor and told all of them to get out of the locker room. Thomas said something and Silo kicked him in the ass. They dragged Rake out of the room and we locked the door."

"For some reason I was crying, and I couldn't stop," Neely said.

Mal had stopped eating. All three were staring straight ahead at the little lady by the stove.

"We found some ice," Paul continued. "Neely said his hand was broken. His nose was bleeding like crazy. He was delirious. Silo was screaming at the team. It was a pretty wild scene."

Mal slurped down some coffee, then tore off a piece of a biscuit, which he dragged across his plate as if he might eat it, or he might not.

"Neely was lying on the floor, ice on his nose, ice on his hand, blood running down his ears. We hated Rake like no man has ever been hated. We wanted to kill somebody, and those poor boys from East Pike were the nearest targets."

After a long pause, Neely said, "Silo knelt beside me and yelled, 'Get your ass up, Mr. All-American. We gotta score five touchdowns.'"

"When Neely got up, we stormed out of the locker room. Rabbit poked his head out of a door, and the last thing I heard was Silo yelling at him, 'Keep those sumbitches away from our sideline.'"

"Hindu threw a bloody towel at him," Neely said, still softly.

"Late in the fourth quarter, Neely and Silo got the team together by the bench and told us that after the game we were running back to the locker room, locking the door, and not coming out until the crowd was gone."

"And we did. We waited in there for a long time," Neely said. "It took an hour just to settle down."

The door opened behind them as one group of locals left while another trooped in.

"And y'all never talked about it?" Mal asked.

"No. We agreed to bury it," Neely said.

"Until now?"

"I guess. Rake's dead, it doesn't matter anymore."

"Why was it such a secret?"

"We were afraid there'd be trouble," Paul said. "We hated Rake, but he was still Rake. He'd punched a player, and not just anybody. Neely's nose was still bleeding after the game."

"And we were so emotional," Neely said. "I think all fifty of us were crying when the game was over. We'd just pulled off a miracle, against impossible odds. With no coaches. Nothing but sheer guts. Just a bunch of kids who'd survived under enormous pressure. We decided it would be our secret. Silo went around the room, looked every player in the eyes and demanded a vow of silence."

"Said he'd kill anyone who ever told," Paul said with chuckle.

Mal skillfully poured a pint of molasses over his next target. "That's a good story. I figured as much."

Paul said, "The odd part is that the coaches never talked about it either. Rabbit kept his mouth shut. Total silence."

Chomp, chomp, then, "We sorta figured it out," Mal said. "Knew something bad happened at halftime. Neely couldn't pass, then word leaked that he was wearing a cast the next week at school. Figured he hit something. Figured it might've been Rake. Lots of rumors over the years, which, as you know, ain't hard to find in Messina."

"I've never heard anyone talk about it," Paul said.

A pull on the coffee. Neither Neely nor Paul were eating or drinking. "Remember that Tugdale kid, from out near Black Rock? A year or two behind you boys."

"Andy Tugdale," Neely said. "Hundred-and-forty-pound guard. Mean as a yard dog."

"That's him. We picked him up years ago for beatin' his wife, had him in jail for a few weeks. I played cards with him, somethin' I always do when we get one of Rake's boys in. I give 'em a special cell, better food, weekend passes."

"The perks of brotherhood," Paul said.

"Somethin' like that. You'll appreciate it when I arrest your little banker's ass."

"Anyway."

"Anyway, we were talkin' one day and I asked Tugdale what happened at halftime during the '87 title game. Clammed up, tight as a tick, not a word. I said I knew there'd been a fight of some sort. Not a word. I waited a few days, tried again. He finally said that Silo had kicked the coaches out of the locker room, told 'em to stay away from the sideline. Said there had been a rather serious disagreement between Rake and Neely. I asked him what Neely had hit to break his hand. A wall? A locker? A chalkboard? None of the above. Somebody else? Bingo. But he wouldn't say who."

"That's great police work, Mal," Paul said. "I might just vote for you next time."

"Can we leave?" Neely said. "I don't like this story."

They rode in silence for half an hour. Still flying with all lights on, Mal appeared to doze occasionally as his ponderous breakfast got digested.

"I'll be happy to drive," Neely said after the car eased onto the gravel shoulder and flung rocks for half a mile.

"Can't. It's illegal," Mal grunted, suddenly wide awake.

Five minutes later he was fading again. Neely decided conversation might keep him awake.

"Did you bust Jesse?" Neely asked as he tightened his seat belt.

"Naw. The state boys got him." Mal shifted his weight and reached for a cigarette. There was a story to tell so he limbered up. "They kicked him off the team at Miami, out of school, barely got out with no jail time, and before long he was back here. Poor guy was hooked on the stuff and couldn't shake it. His family tried everything, rehab, lockdowns, counselors, all that crap. Broke 'em. Hell, it killed his father. The Trapp family once owned two thousand acres of the best farmland around here, now it's all gone. His poor momma lives in that big house with the roof crumblin'."

"Anyway," Paul said helpfully from the rear.

"Anyway, he started sellin' the stuff, and of course Jesse could not be content as a small-timer. He had some contacts in Dade County, one thing led to another and before long he had a nice business. Had his own organization, with lots of ambition."

"Didn't someone get killed?" Paul asked.

"I was gettin' to that," Mal growled at his rearview mirror.

"Just trying to help."

"I always wanted a banker in my backseat. A real white-collar type."

"And I always wanted to foreclose on the Sheriff."

"Truce," Neely said. "You were getting to the good part."

Mal reshifted, his large stomach rubbing the wheel. One more harsh glance into his mirror, then, "The state narcs slowly crept in, as they always do. They nabbed a flunkie, threatened him with thirty years of prison and sodomy, convinced him to flip. He set up a drop with narcs hidin' in the trees and under the rocks. The deal went bad, guns were grabbed, shots went off. A narc took a bullet in the ear and died on the spot. The flunkie got hit, but survived. Jesse was nowhere around, but it was his people. He became a priority, and within a year he was standin' before His Honor receivin' his twenty-eight years, no parole."

"Twenty-eight years," Neely repeated.

"Yep. I was in the courtroom, and I actually felt sorry for the scumbag. I mean, here's a guy who had the tools to play in the NFL. Size, speed, mean as hell, plus Rake had drilled him from the time he was fourteen. Rake always said that if Jesse had gone to A&M, he wouldn't have turned bad. Rake was in the courtroom too."

"How long has he served?" Neely asked.

"Nine, ten years maybe. I ain't countin'. Y'all hungry?"

"We just ate," Neely said.

"Surely you can't be hungry again," Paul said.

"No, but there's this little joint right up here where Miss Armstrong makes pecan fudge. I hate to pass it."

"Let's keep going," Neely said. "Just say no."

"Take it one day at a time, Mal," Paul offered from the rear.

———

The Buford Detention Facility was in flat treeless farmland at the end of a lonely paved road lined with miles of chain-link fencing. Neely was depressed before any building came into sight.

Mal's phone calls had arranged things properly and they were cleared through the front gates and drove deeper into the prison. They changed vehicles at a checkpoint, swapping the roomy patrol car for the narrow benches of an extended golf cart. Mal rode up front where he chatted nonstop with the driver, a guard wearing as much ammunition and gadgets as the Sheriff himself. Neely and Paul shared the back bench, facing the rear, as they passed more chain link and razor wire. They got an eyeful as they puttered past Camp A, a long dismal cinder-block building with prisoners lounging on the front steps. On one side, a basketball game was raging. All the players were black. On the other side, an all-white volleyball game was in progress. Camps B, C, and D were just as bleak. "How could anyone survive in there?" Neely asked himself.

At an intersection, they turned and were soon up at Camp E, which looked somewhat newer. At Camp F they stopped and walked fifty yards to a point where the fencing turned ninety degrees. The guard mumbled something into his radio, then pointed and said, "Walk down that fence to the white pole. He'll be out shortly." Neely and Paul began walking along the fence, where the grass had been recently cut. Mal and the guard held back and lost interest.

Behind the building and beside the basketball court was a slab of concrete, and scattered across it were all sorts of mismatched barbells and bench presses and stacks of dead weights. Some very large black and white men were pumping iron in the morning sun, their bare chests and backs shining with sweat. Evidently, they lifted weights for hours each day.

"There he is," Paul said. "Just getting up from the bench press, on the left."

"That's Jesse," Neely said, mesmerized by a scene that few people ever witnessed.

A trustee approached and said something to Jesse Trapp, who jerked his head and searched the fence line until he saw the two men. He tossed a towel onto a bench and began a slow, purposeful, Spartanlike walk across the slab, across the empty basketball court, and onto the grass that ran to the fence around Camp F.

From forty yards away he looked huge, but as Jesse approached the enormity of his chest and neck and arms became awesome. They had played with him for one season—he was a senior when they were sophomores—and they had seen him naked in the locker room. They had seen him fling heavily loaded barbells around the weight room. They had seen him set every Spartan lifting record.

He looked twice as big now, his neck as thick as an oak stump, his shoulders as wide as a door. His biceps and triceps were many times the normal size. His stomach looked like a cobble-stone street.

He wore a crew cut that made his square head even more symmetrical, and when he stopped and looked down at them he smiled. "Hey boys," he said, still breathing heavily from the last set of reps.

"Hello Jesse," Paul said.

"How are you?" Neely said.

"Doing well, can't complain. Good to see y'all. I don't get many visitors."

"We have bad news, Jesse," Paul said.

"I figured."

"Rake's dead. Passed away last night."

He lowered his chin until it touched his massive chest. From the waist up he seemed to shrink a little as the news hit him. "My mother wrote me and told me he was sick," he said with his eyes closed.

"It was cancer. Diagnosed about a year ago, but the end came pretty fast."

"Man oh man. I thought Rake would live forever."

"I think we all did," Neely said.

Ten years in prison had taught him to control whatever emotions ventured his way. He swallowed hard and opened his eyes. "Thanks for coming. You didn't have to."

"We wanted to see you, Jesse," Neely said. "I think about you all the time."

"The great Neely Crenshaw."

"A long time ago."

"Why don't you write me a letter? I got eighteen more years here."

"I'll do that, Jesse, I promise."

"Thanks."

Paul kicked the grass. "Look, Jesse, there's a memorial service tomorrow, at the field. Most of Rake's boys will be there, you know, to say good-bye. Mal thinks he might be able to pull some strings and get you a pass."

"No way, man."

"You got a lot of friends there, Jesse."

"Former friends, Paul, people I've let down. They'll all point and say, 'Look, there's Jesse Trapp. Coulda been great, but got messed up on drugs. Ruined his life. Learn from him, kids. Stay away from the bad stuff.' No thanks. I don't want to be pointed at."

"Rake would want you there," Neely said.

The chin dropped again and the eyes closed. A moment passed. "I loved Eddie Rake like I've loved nobody else in my life. He was in court the day I got sent away. I had ruined my life, and I was humiliated over that. I had wrecked my parents, and I was sick about that. But what hurt the most was that I had failed in Rake's eyes. It still hurts. Y'all can bury him without me."

"It's your call, Jesse," Paul said.

"Thanks, but I'll pass."

There was a long pause as all three nodded and studied the grass. Finally, Paul said, "I see your mom once a week. She's doing well."

"Thanks. She visits me the third Sunday of every month. You ought to drive over sometime, say hello. It's pretty lonely in here."

"I'll do that, Jesse."

"You promise?"

"I promise. And I wish you'd think about tomorrow."

"I've already thought about it. I'll say a prayer for Rake, you boys can bury him."

"Fair enough."

Jesse looked to his right. "Is that Mal over there?"

"Yes, we rode with him."

"Tell him to kiss my ass."

"I'll do that, Jesse," Paul said. "With pleasure."

"Thanks boys," Jesse said. He turned and walked away.

———————

At four o'clock Thursday afternoon the crowd parted at the gate to Rake Field and the hearse backed itself into position. Its rear door was opened and eight pallbearers formed two short lines and pulled out the casket. None of the eight were former Spartans. Eddie Rake had given much thought to his final details, and he had decided not to play favorites. He selected his pallbearers from among his assistant coaches.

The procession moved slowly around the track. The casket was followed by Mrs. Lila Rake, her three daughters and their husbands, and a handsome collection of grandchildren. Then a priest. Then the drum corps from the Spartan marching band, doing a soft roll as they passed the home stands.

Between the forties on the home sideline

there was a large white tent, its poles anchored in buckets of sand to protect the sacred Bermuda of Rake Field. At the fifty-yard line, at the exact spot where he had coached for so long and so well, they stopped with his casket. It was mounted on an antique Irish wake table, the property of Lila's best friend, and quickly surrounded by flowers. When the Coach was properly arranged, the family gathered around the casket for a short prayer. Then they formed a receiving line.

The line stretched down the track and through the gate, and the cars were bumper to bumper on the road that led to Rake Field.

———

Neely passed the house three times before he was brave enough to stop. There was a rental car in the driveway. Cameron had returned. Long after dinner, he knocked on the door, almost as nervous as the first time he'd done so. Then, as a fifteen-year-old with a new driver's permit, his parents' car, twenty bucks in his pocket, the peach fuzz scraped off his face, he had arrived to take Cameron on their first real date.

A hundred years ago.

Mrs. Lane opened the door, same as always, but this time she did not recognize Neely. "Good evening," she said softly. She was still beautiful, polite, refusing to age.

"Mrs. Lane, it's me, Neely Crenshaw."

As the words came out, she recognized him. "Why, yes, Neely, how are you?"

He figured his name had been mud in the house for so long, he wasn't sure how he'd be received. But the Lanes were gracious people, slightly more educated and affluent than most in Messina. If they held a grudge, and he was certain one was being held, they wouldn't show it. Not the parents anyway.

"I'm fine," he said.

"Would you come in?" she said, opening the door. It was a halfhearted gesture.

"Sure, thanks." In the foyer, he looked around and said, "Still a beautiful home, Mrs. Lane."

"Thank you. Could I get you some tea?"

"No, thanks. Actually, I'm looking for Cameron. Is she here?"

"She is."

"I'd like to say hello."

"I'm very sorry about Coach Rake. I know he meant everything to you boys."

"Yes ma'am." He was glancing around, listening for voices in the back of the house.

"I'll find Cameron," she said and disappeared. Neely waited, and waited, and finally turned to the large oval window in the front door and watched the dark street.

There was a footstep behind him, then a familiar voice. "Hello Neely," Cameron said. He turned and they stared at each other. Words failed him for the moment, so he shrugged and finally blurted, "I was just driving by, thought I'd say hello. It's been a long time."

"It has."

The gravity of his mistake hit hard.

She was much prettier than in high school. Her thick auburn hair was pulled back into a ponytail. Her dark blue eyes were adorned with chic designer frames. She wore a bulky cotton sweater and tight faded jeans that declared that this was a lady who stayed in shape. "You look great," he said as he admired her.

"You too."

"Can we talk?"

"About what?"

"Life, love, football. There's a good chance we'll never see each other again, and I have something to say."

She opened the door. They walked across the wide porch and sat on the front steps. She was careful to leave a large gap between them. Five minutes passed in silence.

"I saw Nat," he said. "He told me you're living in Chicago, happily married with two little girls."

"True."

"Who'd you marry?"

"Jack."

"Jack who?"

"Jack Seawright."

"Where'd he come from?"

"I met him in D.C. I went to work there after college."

"How old are your girls?"

"Five and three."

"What does Jack do?"

"Bagels."

"Bagels?"

"Yes, those round things. We didn't have bagels in Messina."

"Okay. You mean, like, a bagel shop?"

"Shops."

"More than one?"

"A hundred and forty-six."

"So you're doing well?"

"His company is worth eight million."

"Ouch. My little company is worth twelve thousand on a good day."

"You said you had something to say." She had shown not the slightest hint of thawing. There was no interest in any of the details of his life.

Neely heard faint footsteps on the wooden floor of the foyer. No doubt Mrs. Lane was back there, trying to listen. Some things never changed.

The wind picked up slightly and scattered oak leaves across the brick sidewalk in front of them. Neely rubbed his hands together and said, "Okay, here goes. A long time ago, I did a very bad thing, something I've been ashamed of for many years. I was wrong. It was stupid, mean, lousy, selfish, harmful, and the older I get the more I regret it. I'm apologizing, Cameron, and I ask you to forgive me."

"You're forgiven. Forget about it."

"I can't forget about it. And don't be so nice."

"We were just kids, Neely. Sixteen years old. It was another lifetime."

"We were in love, Cameron. I adored you from the time we were ten years old and holding hands behind the gym so the other boys wouldn't see me."

"I really don't want to hear this."

"Okay, but can I get it off my chest? And would you try to make it painful?"

"I got over it, Neely, finally."

"Maybe I haven't."

"Oh get a life! And grow up while you're at it. You're not the football hero anymore."

"There you go. That's what I want to hear. Unload with both barrels."

"Did you come here to fight, Neely?"

"No. I came to say I'm sorry."

"You've said it. Now why don't you leave?"

He bit his tongue and let a few seconds pass. Then, "Why do you want me to leave?"

"Because I don't like you, Neely."

"You shouldn't."

"It took ten years to get you out of my system. When I fell in love with Jack, I was finally able to forget you. I hoped I would never see you again."

"Do you ever think about me?"

"No."

"Never?"

"Maybe once a year, in a weak moment. Jack was watching a football game once. The quarterback got hurt and left the game on a stretcher. I thought of you then."

"A pleasant thought."

"Not unpleasant."

"I think of you all the time."

A slight crack in the ice as she exhaled and seemed frustrated. She leaned forward and rested both elbows on her knees. The door opened behind them and Mrs. Lane shuffled out with a tray. "Thought you might like some hot chocolate," she said, placing it on the edge of the porch, in the large space between them.

"Thank you," Neely said.

"It'll keep the chill off," Mrs. Lane said. "Cameron, you should put on some socks."

"Yes, Mother."

The door closed and they ignored the hot chocolate. Neely wanted a long conversation, one that covered several issues and many years. She once had feelings, strong ones, and he wanted to confirm them. He wanted tears and anger, maybe a good fight or two. And he wanted to be truly forgiven.

"You were actually watching a football game?" he said.

"No. Jack was watching the game. I happened to be passing through."

"He's a football fan?"

"Not really. If he'd been a fan, I wouldn't have married him."

"So you still hate football?"

"You could say that. I went to Hollins, an all-girls school, so I could avoid football. My oldest daughter has started school at a small private academy—no football."

"Then why are you here now?"

"Miss Lila. She taught me piano for twelve years."

"Right."

"I'm certainly not here to honor Eddie Rake." Cameron picked up a cup and cradled it with both hands. Neely did the same.

When it became apparent he was in no hurry to leave, she opened up a little. "I had a sorority sister at Hollins whose brother played for State. She was watching a game, our sophomore year, and I walked into her room. There was the great Neely Crenshaw, moving Tech up and down the field, fans going wild, the announcers giddy over this great young quarterback. I thought, 'Well, good. That's what he always wanted. A big-time hero. Adoring masses. Coeds chasing him all over campus, throwing themselves at him. Constant adulation. Everybody's all-American. That's Neely.' "

"Two weeks later I was in the hospital."

She shrugged. "I didn't know. I wasn't following your great career."

"Who told you?"

"I was home for Christmas break, and I had lunch with Nat. He told me you'd never play again. It's such a stupid sport. Boys and young men mangle their bodies for life."

"It is indeed."

"So tell me, Neely, what happened to the girls? When you're no longer the hero, what happens to all those little sluts and groupies?"

"They disappear."

"That must've killed you."

"Now we're making progress," Neely thought. "Let's get the venom out."

"There was nothing pleasant about the injury."

"So you became just a regular person, like the rest of us?"

"I guess, but with a lot of baggage. Being a forgotten hero is not easy."

"And you're still adjusting?"

"When you're famous at eighteen, you spend the rest of your life fading away. You dream of the glory days, but you know they're gone forever. I wish I'd never seen a football."

"I don't believe that."

"I'd be a regular guy with two good legs. And I wouldn't have made the mistake with you."

"Oh please, Neely, don't get sappy. We were only sixteen."

Another long pause as they sipped from their cups and got ready for the next serve and volley. Neely had been planning the encounter for weeks. Cameron had had no idea she would ever see him again. Still, he knew the element of surprise would not help him. She would have all the answers.

"You're not saying much," he said.

"I have nothing to say."

"Come on, Cameron, this is your chance to unload with both barrels."

"Why should I? You're here trying to force me to dig up bad memories that took years to forget. What makes you think I want to go back to high school and get burned again? I've dealt with it, Neely. Obviously you haven't."

"You want to know about Screamer?"

"Hell no."

"She's a cocktail waitress at a low rent casino in Vegas, fat and ugly, thirty-two and looking fifty, all according to Paul Curry, who saw her there. Apparently she went to Hollywood, tried to sleep her way to the top, got squeezed out by a million other small-town homecoming queens trying to sleep their way to the top."

"No surprise."

"Paul said she looked tired."

"I'm certain of that. She looked tired in high school."

"Does that make you feel better?"

"I felt great before you got here, Neely. I have no interest in you or your homecoming queen."

"Come on, Cameron. Be honest. It must be somewhat satisfying to know that Screamer is closing in on skid row while your life is looking pretty good. You've won."

"I wasn't competing. I don't care."

"You cared back then."

She placed the cup back on the tray and leaned forward again. "What do you want me to say, Neely? Shall I state the obvious? I loved you madly when I was a young teenage girl. That's no surprise because I told you every day. And you told me the same. We spent every moment together, had every class together, went everywhere together. But you became this great football hero, and everybody wanted a piece of you. Especially Screamer. She had the long legs and cute butt and short skirts and big chest and blond hair, and somehow she got you in the backseat of her car. You decided you wanted more of the same. I was a nice girl, and I paid a price for it. You broke my heart, humiliated me in front of everybody I knew, and wrecked my life for a long time. I couldn't wait to leave this town."

"I still can't believe I did that."

"Well, you did." Her voice was edgy and there was a slight crack. She clenched her teeth, determined to show no emotion. He would not make her cry again.

"I'm so sorry." Neely slowly got to his feet, careful not to put too much weight on his left knee. He touched her on the arm and said, "Thanks for giving me the chance to say so."

"Don't mention it."

"Good-bye."

He walked down the sidewalk with a slight limp, through the gate. When he was near his car, she called out, "Neely, wait."

Because of his high-voltage romance with Brandy Skimmel, aka Screamer, now also known, by a very few, as Tessa Canyon, Neely knew all the back alleys and deserted streets of Messina. He circled

Karr's Hill, where they paused for a moment to look down at the football field. The line of well-wishers still ran along the track and out the front gate. The lights on the home side were on. The parking lot was full of cars coming and going.

"They say Rake would sit up here, after they fired him, and watch the games."

"They should've put him in jail," Cameron said, her first and only words since leaving home.

They parked near a practice field and sneaked through a gate on the visitors' side. They climbed to the top of the bleachers and sat down, still with a gap between them, though closer than on her front porch. For a long time they watched the scene on the other side of the field.

The white tent rose like a small pyramid in front of the home stands. The casket was barely visible under it. A crowd was gathered around, enjoying the vigil. Miss Lila and the family had left. Racks of flowers were accumulating around the tent and up and down the sideline. A silent parade of mourners inched along the track, patiently waiting for the chance to sign the regis- ter, see the casket, perhaps shed a tear, and say farewell to their legend. Up in the stands behind the line of people, Rake's boys of all ages were grouped in small packs, some talking, some laughing, most just staring at the field and the tent and the casket.

Only two people were in the visitors' stands, unnoticed.

Cameron spoke first, very softly. "Who are those people up in the bleachers?"

"Players. I was up there last night and the night before, waiting for Rake to die."

"So they're all coming home?"

"Most of us. You came home."

"Of course. We're burying our most famous citizen."

"You didn't like Rake, did you?"

"I was not a fan. Miss Lila is a strong woman, but she was no match for him. He was a dictator on the field, and he had trouble turning it off when he got home. No, I didn't care for Eddie Rake."

"You hated football."

"I hated you, and that made me hate football."

"Atta girl."

"It was silly. Grown men crying after a loss. The entire town living and dying with each game. Prayer breakfasts every Friday morning, as if God cares who wins a high school football game. More money spent on the football team than on all other student groups combined. Worshiping seventeen-year-old boys who quickly become convinced they are truly worthy of being worshiped. The double standard—a football player cheats on a test, everybody scrambles to cover it up. A nonathlete cheats, and he gets suspended. The stupid little girls who can't wait to give it up to a Spartan. All for the good of the team. Messina needs its young virgins to sacrifice everything. Oh, and I almost forgot. The Pep Girls! Each player gets his own little slave who bakes him cookies on Wednesday and puts a spirit sign in his front yard on Thursday and polishes his helmet on Friday and what do you get on Saturday, Neely, a quickie?"

"Only if you want it."

"It's a sad scene. Thank you for shoving me out of it."

Looking back with the clear hindsight of fifteen years, it did indeed seem silly.

"But you came to the games," Neely said.

"A few of them. You have any idea what this town is like on Friday night away from the field? There's not a soul anywhere. Phoebe Cox and I would sneak over here, on the visitors' side and watch the games. We always wanted Messina to lose, but it never happened, not here. We ridiculed the band and the cheerleaders and the Pep Squad and everything else, and we did so because we were not a part of it. I couldn't wait to get to college."

"I knew you were up here."

"No you didn't."

"I swear. I knew."

Faint laughter drifted across the field as another Rake story found its mark among his boys. Neely could barely make out Silo and Paul in a group of ten others just under the press box. The beer was flowing.

"After you took the plunge in the backseat," she said, "and I was tossed aside, we still had two years left in this place. There were moments when I would see you in the hall, or the library, or even in the classroom, and our eyes would meet, just for a second. Gone was the cocky sneer, the arrogant look of everybody's hero. Just for a split-second you would look at me like a real person, and I would know that you still cared. I would've taken you back in a heartbeat."

"And I wanted you."

"That's hard to believe."

"It's true."

"But, of course, the joy of sex."

"I couldn't help myself."

"Congratulations, Neely. You and Screamer began your adventures at the age of sixteen. Look at her now. Fat and tired."

"Did you ever hear the rumor that she was pregnant?"

"Are you kidding? Rumors are like mosquitoes in this town."

"The summer before our senior year, she tells me she's pregnant."

"What a surprise. Basic biology."

"So we drove to Atlanta, got an abortion, drove back to Messina. I swear I never told a soul."

"Rested twenty-four hours, then back in the rut."

"Close."

"Look, Neely, I'm really tired of your sex life. It was my curse for many years. Either change the subject, or I'm out of here."

Another long awkward pause as they watched the receiving line and thought about what to say next. A breeze blew in their faces and she held her arms close to her chest. He fought the desire to reach over and hold her. It wouldn't work.

"You've asked nothing about my life these days," he said.

"I'm sorry. I stopped thinking about you a long time ago. I can't lie, Neely. You're just not a factor anymore."

"You were always blunt."

"Blunt is good. It saves so much time."

"I sell real estate, live alone with a dog, date a girl I really don't like, date another one with two children, and I really miss my ex-wife."

"What caused the divorce?"

"She cracked up. She miscarried twice, the second one in the fourth month. I made the mistake of telling her I once paid for an abortion, so she blamed me for losing the babies. She was right. The real cost of an abortion is much more than the lousy three hundred bucks at the clinic."

"I'm sorry."

"Ten years to the week after Screamer and I made our little road trip to Atlanta, my wife had the second miscarriage. A little boy."

"I really want to leave now."

"I'm sorry."

They sat on the front steps again. The lights were off. Mr. and Mrs. Lane were asleep. It was after eleven. "I think you should go now," Cameron said after a few minutes.

"You're right."

"You said earlier that you think about me all the time now. I'm curious as to why."

"I had no idea how painful a broken heart can be until my wife packed up and left. It was a nightmare. For the first time, I realized what you had suffered through. I realized how cruel I had been."

"You'll get over it. Takes about ten years."

"Thanks."

He walked down the sidewalk, then turned around and walked back. "How old is Jack?" he asked.

"Thirty-seven."

"Then, statistically, he should die first. Give me a call when he's gone. I'll be waiting."

"Sure you will."

"I swear. Isn't it comforting to know that someone will always be waiting for you?"

"I hadn't thought about it."

He leaned down and looked her in the eyes. "Can I kiss you on the cheek?"

"No."

"There's something magical about the first love, Cameron, something I'll miss forever."

"Good-bye Neely."

"Can I say I love you?"

"No. Good-bye Neely."

Friday

Messina mourned like never before. By ten on Friday morning the shops and cafés and offices around the square were locked. All students were dismissed from school. The courthouse was closed. The factories on the edges of the town were shut down, a free holiday, though few felt like celebrating.

Mal Brown placed his deputies around the high school, where by mid-morning the traffic was bumper to bumper on the road to Rake Field.

By eleven, the home stands were almost full, and the ex-players, the former heroes, were gathering and milling around the tent at the fifty-yard line. Most of them wore their green game jerseys, a gift to every senior. And most jerseys were stretched tighter around the midsections. A few—the lawyers and doctors and bankers—wore sports coats over their game shirts, but the green was visible.

From the bleachers up above the fans looked down at the tent and the field and enjoyed the chance to identify their old heroes. Those with retired numbers caused the most excitement. "There's Roman Armstead, number 81, played for the Packers." "There's Neely, number 19."

The senior class string quartet played under the tent and the P.A. system lifted its sounds from end zone to end zone. The town kept coming.

There would be no casket. Eddie Rake was already in the ground. Miss Lila and her family arrived without ceremony and spent half an hour hugging former players in front of the tent. Just before noon, the priest appeared, and then a choir, but the crowd was far from settled. When the home bleachers were full, they began lining the fence around the track. There was no hurry. This was a moment Messina would cherish and remember.

Rake wanted his boys on the field, packed around the small podium near the edge of the tent. And he wanted them to wear their jerseys, a request that had been quietly spread in his last days. A tarp covered the track and several hundred folding chairs had been arranged in a half-moon. Around twelve-thirty, Father McCabe gave the signal and the players began packing into their seats. Miss Lila and the family sat in the front rows.

Neely was between Paul Curry and Silo Mooney, with thirty other members of the 1987 team around them. Two were dead and six had disappeared. The rest couldn't make it.

A bagpipe at the north goalpost began wailing and the crowd became still. Silo was wiping tears almost immediately, and he was not alone. As the last melancholy notes drifted across the field, the mourners were softened up and ready for some serious emotion. Father McCabe slowly approached the makeshift podium and adjusted the microphone.

"Good afternoon," he said in a high-pitched voice that broke sharply through the stadium speakers and could be heard half a mile away. "And welcome to our celebration of the life of Eddie Rake. On behalf of Mrs. Lila Rake, her three daughters, eight grandchildren, and the rest of the family, I welcome you and say thank you for coming."

He flipped a page of notes. "Carl Edward Rake was born seventy-two years ago in Gaithersburg, Maryland. Forty-eight years ago he married the former Lila Saunders. Forty-four years ago he was hired by the Messina School Board as the head football Coach. At the time he was twenty-eight, had no head coaching experience, and always said he got the job because no one else wanted it. He coached here for thirty-four years, won over four hundred games, thirteen state titles, and we know the rest of the numbers. More important, he touched the lives of all of us. Coach Rake died Wednesday night. He was buried this morning in a private ceremony, family only, and at his personal request, and with the consent of the Reardon family, he was laid to rest beside Scotty. Coach Rake told me last week that he was dreaming of Scotty, said he couldn't wait to see him up in heaven, to hold him and hug him and tell him he was sorry."

With perfect timing, he paused to allow this to choke up the crowd. He opened a Bible.

As he was about to speak, there was a commotion near the front gate. A loud radio squawked. Car doors slammed and there were voices. People were scrambling around. Father McCabe paused and looked, and this caused everyone else to look too.

A giant of a man was walking briskly through the gate, onto the track. It was Jesse Trapp, with a prison guard at each elbow. He was wearing perfectly pressed khaki pants and shirt, prison issue, and the handcuffs had been removed. His guards were in uniform, and not much smaller. The crowd froze when they recognized him. As he walked along the sideline his head was high, his back stiff, a proud man, but he also had a look of slight bewilderment. Where should he sit? Would he fit? Would he be welcome? As he approached the end of the stands, someone in the crowd caught his attention. A voice called out, and Jesse stopped cold.

It was his mother, a tiny woman holding a place along the fence. He lunged for her and hugged her tightly over the chain-link as his guards glanced at each other to make sure that, yes, it was okay for their prisoner to hug his mother.

From a wrinkled grocery bag, Mrs. Trapp pulled out a green jersey. Number 56, retired in 1985. Jesse held it and looked down the track at the former players, all straining to see him. In front of the same ten thousand people who once screamed for him to maim opposing players, he quickly unbuttoned his shirt and took it off. Suddenly, he exposed more brilliantly toned and tanned muscles than anyone had ever seen, and he seemed to pause so they, and he, could enjoy the moment. Father McCabe waited patiently, and so did everyone else.

When he had the jersey arranged just so, he pulled it over his head, then tugged here and there until it was properly in place. It strained over the biceps and was very tight across the chest and around the neck, but every other Spartan there would've killed to fill it so well. It was loose at the narrow waist, and when he carefully tucked it into his pants the jersey looked as if it might burst open. He hugged his mother again.

Someone applauded, then several people stood, clapping. Welcome home, Jesse, we still love you. Quickly, the bleachers rattled as people rose to their feet. A thunderous wave of applause engulfed Rake Field as the town embraced a fallen hero. Jesse nodded, then waved awkwardly as he continued his slow walk to the podium. The standing ovation grew louder as he shook hands with Father McCabe and hugged Miss Lila. He hugged his way through a haphazard aisle of former players, and finally found an empty folding chair that seemed to sink under his weight. By the time Jesse was seated and still, tears were dripping from his face.

Father McCabe waited until all was quiet again. There would be no rush on this day, no one was watching the clock. He adjusted the mike again and said, "One of Coach Rake's favorite Scripture verses was the Twenty-Third Psalm. We read it together last Monday. His favorite lines were, 'Yea, though I walk through the valley of the shadow of death, I will fear no evil . . . thy rod and thy staff they comfort me.' Eddie Rake lived his life with no fear. His players were taught that those who are timid and frightened have no place among the victors. Those who take no risks receive no rewards. A few months ago, Coach Rake accepted the reality that his death was inevitable. He was unafraid of his disease and the suffering that would follow. He was unafraid of saying good-bye to those he loved. He was unafraid of dying. His faith in God was strong and unshakable. 'Death is just the beginning,' he liked to say."

Father McCabe bowed slightly and backed away from the podium. On cue, an all-female choir from a black church began humming. They wore scarlet and gold robes, and, after a short warm-up, launched into a boisterous rendition of "Amazing Grace." The music stirred emotions, as it always does on such occasions. And memories. Every Spartan player was soon lost in his own images of Eddie Rake.

For Neely, thoughts of Rake always began with the slap in the face, the broken nose, the punch that knocked out his Coach, and the dramatic comeback for the state title. And he always fought himself to move on, to get past that painful moment and recapture the good times.

Rare is the Coach who can motivate players to spend their lives seeking his approval. From the time Neely first put on a uniform in the sixth grade, he wanted Rake's attention. And in the next six years, with every pass he threw, every drill he ran, every play he memorized, every weight he lifted, every hour he spent sweating, every pregame speech he gave, every touchdown he scored, every game he won, every temptation he resisted, every honor roll he made, he coveted Eddie Rake's approval. He wanted to see Rake's face when he won the Heisman. He dreamed of Rake's phone call when Tech won the national title.

And rare is the Coach who compounds every failure long after the playing days are over. When the doctors told Neely he would never play again, he felt as if he had fallen short of Rake's ambitions for him. When his marriage dissolved, he could almost see Rake's disapproving scowl. As his small-time real estate career drifted with no clear ambition, he knew Rake would have a lecture if he got close enough to hear it.

Maybe his death would kill the demon that dogged him, but he had his doubts.

Ellen Rake Young, the eldest daughter, walked to the podium when the choir was finished and unfolded a sheet of paper. Like her sisters, she had wisely fled Messina after high school, and returned only when family matters required. Her father's shadow was too mammoth for his children to survive in such a small place. She was in her mid-forties, a psychiatrist in Boston, and had the air of someone who was out of place.

"On behalf of our family, I thank you for your prayers and support during these last weeks. My father died with a great deal of courage and dignity. Though his last years here were not some of his best, he loved this town and its people, and he especially loved his players."

Love was not a word any of the players had ever heard their Coach use. If he'd loved them, he'd had a strange way of showing it.

"My father has written a short note that he asked me to read." She adjusted her reading glasses, cleared her throat, and focused on the sheet of paper. "This is Eddie Rake, speaking from the grave. If you are crying, please stop." This brought scattered laughter from the crowd, which was anxious for a light moment. "I've never had any use for tears. My life is now complete, so don't cry for me. And don't cry for the memories. Never look back, there's too much left to do. I'm a lucky man who lived a wonderful life. I had the good sense to marry Lila as soon as I could talk her into it, and God blessed us with three beautiful daughters, and, at last count, eight perfect grandchildren. This alone is enough for any man. But God had many blessings in store for me. He led me to football, and to Messina, my home. And there I met you, my friends, and my players. Though I was emotionally unable to convey my feelings, I want my players to know that I cherished every one of them. Why would any sane person coach high school football for thirty-four years? For me it was easy. I loved my players. I wish I had been able to say so, but it was simply not my nature. We accomplished much, but I will not dwell on the victories and the championships. Instead, I choose this moment to offer two regrets." Ellen paused here and cleared her throat again. The crowd appeared to hold its collective breath. "Only two regrets in thirty-four years. As I said, I'm a lucky man. The first is Scotty Reardon. I never dreamed I would be responsible for the death of one of my players, but I accept the blame for his death. Holding him in my arms as he passed away is something I have wept over every day since. I have expressed these feelings to his parents, and, with time, I think they have forgiven me. I cling to their forgiveness and take it to my death. I am with Scotty now, and for eternity, and as we look down together at this moment we have reconciled our past." Another pause as Ellen took a sip of water. "The second involves the state title game in 1987. At halftime, in a fit of rage, I physically assaulted a player, our quarterback. It was a criminal act, one that should have had me banned from the game forever. I am sorry for my actions. As I watched that team rally against enormous odds, I have never felt such pride, and such pain. That victory was my finest hour. Please forgive me, boys."

Neely glanced around him. All heads were low, most eyes were closed. Silo was wiping his face.

"Enough of the negative. My love to Lila and the girls and the grandkids. We'll all meet very soon across the river, in the promised land. May God be with you."

The choir sang "Just a Closer Walk with Thee," and the tears were flowing.

Neely couldn't help but wonder if Cameron was keeping her emotions in check. He suspected that she was.

Rake had asked three of his former players to deliver eulogies. Short ones, he had demanded in writing from his deathbed. The first was given by the Honorable Mike Hilliard, now a circuit court judge in a small town a hundred miles away. Unlike most of the former Spartans, he wore a suit, one with wrinkles, and a crooked bow tie. He grabbed the podium with both hands and didn't need notes.

"I played on Coach Rake's first team in 1958," he began in a squeaky voice with a thick drawl. "The year before we had won three games and lost seven, which, back then, was considered a good season because we beat Porterville in our final game. The Coach left town and took his assistants with him, and for a while we weren't sure we would find anyone to coach us. They hired this young guy named Eddie Rake, who wasn't much older than we were. The first thing he told us was that we were a bunch of losers, that losing is contagious, that if we thought we could lose with him then we could hit the door. Forty-one of us signed up for football that year. Coach Rake took us off to an old church camp over in Page County for August drills, and after four days the squad was down to thirty. After a week we were down to twenty-five and some of us were beginning to wonder if we'd survive long enough to field a team. The practices were beyond brutal. The bus for Messina left every afternoon, and we were free to get on it. After two weeks the bus was empty and it stopped running. The boys who quit came home telling horror stories of what was happening at Camp Rake, as it was soon called. Our parents were alarmed. My mother told me later she felt like I was off at war. Unfortunately, I've seen war. And I would prefer it over Camp Rake.

"We broke camp with twenty-one players, twenty-one kids who'd never been in such great shape. We were small and slow and didn't have a quarterback, but we were convinced. Our first game was at home against Fulton, a team that had embarrassed us the year before. I'm sure some of you remember it. We led twenty to nothing at halftime and Rake cussed us because we'd made some mistakes. His genius was simple— stick to the basics, and work nonstop until you can execute them perfectly. Lessons I have never forgotten. We won the game, and we were celebrating in the locker room when Rake walked in and told us to shut up. Evidently our execution had not been perfect. He told us to keep our gear on, and after the crowd left we came back to this field and practiced until midnight. We ran two plays until all eleven guys got everything perfect. Our girlfriends were waiting. Our parents were waiting. It was nice to win the game, but folks were beginning to think Coach Rake was crazy. The players already knew it.

"We won eight games that year, lost only two, and the legend of Eddie Rake was born. My senior year we lost one game, then in 1960 Coach Rake had his first undefeated season. I was away at college and I couldn't get home every Friday, though I desperately wanted to. When you play for Rake you join an exclusive little club, and you follow the teams that come behind you. For the next thirty-two years I followed Spartan football as closely as possible. I was here, sitting up there in the bleachers, when the great streak began in '64, and I was at South Wayne when it ended in 1970. Along with you, I watched the great ones play—Wally Webb, Roman Armstead, Jesse Trapp, Neely Crenshaw.

"On the walls of my cluttered office hang the photos of all thirty-four of Rake's teams. He would send me a picture of the team every year. Often, when I should be working, I'll light my pipe and stand before them and look at the faces of all the young men he coached. Skinny white boys in the 1950s, with crew cuts and innocent smiles. Shaggier ones in the 1960s, fewer smiles, determined looks, you can almost see the ominous clouds of war and civil rights in their faces. Black and white players smiling together in the seventies and eighties, much bigger kids, with fancier uniforms, some were the sons of boys I played with. I know that every player looking down from my walls was indelibly touched by Eddie Rake. They ran the same plays, heard the same pep talks, got the same lectures, endured the same brutal drills in August. And every one of us at some time became convinced that we truly hated Eddie Rake. But then we were gone. Our pictures hang on the walls, and we spend the rest of our lives hearing the sound of his voice in the locker room, longing for the days when we called him Coach.

"Most of those faces are here today. Slightly older, grayer, some a bit heavier. All sadder as we say good-bye to Coach Rake. And why do we care? Why are we here? Why are the stands once again filled and overflowing? Well, I will tell you why.

"Few of us will ever do anything that will be recognized and remembered by more than a handful of people. We are not great. We may be good, honest, fair, hardworking, loyal, kind, generous, and very decent, or we may be otherwise. But we are not considered great. Greatness comes along so rarely that when we see it we want to touch it. Eddie Rake allowed us, players and fans, to touch greatness, to be a part of it. He was a great coach who built a great program and a great tradition and gave us all something great, something we will always cherish. Hopefully, most of us will live long happy lives, but we will never again be this close to greatness. That's why we're here.

"Whether you loved Eddie Rake or you didn't, you cannot deny his greatness. He was the finest man I've ever met. My happiest memories are of wearing the green jersey and playing for him on this field. I long for those days. I can hear his voice, feel his wrath, smell his sweat, see his pride. I will always miss the great Eddie Rake."

He paused, then bowed, and abruptly backed away from the microphone as a light, almost awkward applause crept through the crowd. As soon as he sat down, a thick-chested black gentleman in a gray suit stood and marched with great dignity to the podium. Under his jacket was the green jersey. He looked up and gazed upon the crowd packed tightly together.

"Good afternoon," he announced with a voice that needed no microphone. "I'm Reverend Collis Suggs, of the Bethel Church of God in Christ, here in Messina."

Collis Suggs needed no introduction to anyone who lived within fifty miles of Messina.

Eddie Rake had appointed him as the first black captain in 1970. He played briefly at Florida A&M before breaking a leg, then became a minister. He built a large congregation and became involved politically. For years it had been said that if Eddie Rake and Collis Suggs wanted you elected, then you got elected. If not, then take your name off the ballot.

Thirty years in the pulpit had honed his speaking skills to perfection. His diction was perfect, his timing and pitch were captivating. Coach Rake was known to sneak into the rear pew of the Bethel church on Sunday nights just to hear his former noseguard preach.

"I played for Coach Rake in '69 and '70." Most of those in the crowd had seen every game.

"In late July 1969, the U.S. Supreme Court had finally had enough. Fifteen years after *Brown* versus *Board of Education*, and most schools in the South were still segregated. The Court took drastic action, and it changed our lives forever. One hot summer night, we were playing basketball in the gym at Section High, the colored school, when Coach Thomas walked in and said, 'Boys, we're goin' to Messina High School. You're gonna be Spartans. Get on the bus.' About a dozen of us loaded on the bus, and Coach Thomas drove us across town. We were confused and scared. We had been told many times that the schools would be integrated, but deadlines had come and gone. We knew Messina High had the finest of everything—beautiful buildings, nice fields, a huge gym, lots of trophies, a football team that had won, at that time, something like fifty or sixty straight. And they had a coach who thought he was Vince Lombardi. Yes, we were intimidated, but we knew we had to be brave. We arrived at Messina High that night. The football team was lifting weights in this huge weight room, more weights than I had ever seen in my life. About forty guys pumping iron, sweating, music going. As soon as we walked in, everything was quiet. They looked at us. We looked at them. Eddie Rake walked over, shook hands with Coach Thomas, and said, 'Welcome to your new school.' He made us all shake hands, then he sat us down on the mats and gave us a little speech. He said he didn't care what color we were. All his players wore green. His playing field was perfectly level. Hard work won games, and he didn't believe in losing. I remember sitting there on that rubber mat, mesmerized by this man. He immediately became my Coach. Eddie Rake was many things, but he was the greatest motivator I've ever met. I wanted to put on the pads and start hitting people right then.

"Two weeks later we started two-a-day practices in August, and I have never hurt so much in my life. Rake was right. Skin color didn't matter. He treated us all like dogs, equally.

"There was a lot of concern about the first day of classes, about fights and racial conflict. And most schools saw a lot of it. Not here. The principal put Coach Rake in charge of security, and everything went smoothly. He put all of his players in green game jerseys, same ones we're wearing right now, and he paired us up, a black player with a white player. When the buses rolled in, we were there to greet them. The first thing the black kids saw at Messina High was the football team, black and white players together, everybody wearing green. A couple of hotheads wanted some trouble, but we convinced them otherwise.

"The first controversy was over the

cheerleaders. The white girls had been practicing all summer as a squad. Coach Rake went to the principal and said half and half would work just fine. And it did. Still does. Next came the band. There wasn't enough money to combine the white band and the black band and have every-body march in Messina uniforms. Some kids would get cut. It looked like most of those left on the sideline would be black. Coach Rake went to the booster club, said he needed twenty thousand dollars for new band uniforms. Said Messina would have the largest high school marching band in the state, and we still do.

"There was a lot of resistance to integration. Many white folks thought it was only temporary. Once the courts got finished, then everything would revert back to the old system of separate but equal. I'm here to tell you, separate was never equal. There was a lot of speculation on our side of town about whether the white coaches would actually play us black kids. And there was a lot of pressure from the white side of town to play white kids only. After three weeks of practice with Eddie Rake, we knew the truth. Our first game that year was against North Delta. They hit the field all-white. Had about fifteen black guys on the bench. I knew some of them, knew they could play. Rake put the best players on the field, and we soon realized that North Delta did not. It was a slaughter. At halftime, we were leading forty-one to nothing. When the second half started, the black kids came off the bench for North Delta, and, I have to admit, we relaxed a little. Problem was, nobody relaxed with Eddie Rake. If he caught you loafing on the field, then you got to stay on the sideline with him.

"Word spread that Messina was starting their black kids, and soon the issue was settled all over the state.

"Eddie Rake was the first white man who ever yelled at me and made me like it. Once I realized that he truly did not care about the color of my skin, then I knew I would follow him anywhere. He hated injustice. Because he wasn't from here, he brought a different perspective. No person had the right to mistreat another, and if Coach Rake got wind of it then a fight was coming. For all of his toughness, he was terribly sensitive to the suffering of others. After I became a minister, Coach Rake would come to our church and work in our outreach programs. He opened his home to abandoned and abused children. He never made much money as a Coach, but he was generous when someone needed food or clothing or even tuition. He coached youth teams in the summer. Of course, knowing Rake, he was also looking for the boys who could run. He organized fishing rodeos for kids with no fathers. Typically, he never sought recognition for any of this."

The reverend took a pause and a sip of water. The crowd watched every move and waited.

"After they fired Coach Rake, I spent some time with him. He was convinced that he had been treated unfairly. But as the years went by, I think Coach accepted his fate. I know he grieved over Scotty Reardon. And I'm so happy that he was laid to rest this morning next to Scotty. Maybe now this town can stop the feuding. How ironic that the man who put us on the map, the man who did so much to bring so many together, was also the man that Messina has been fighting over for ten years now. Let's all bury the hatchet, lay down our arms, and make peace over Eddie Rake. We are all one in Christ. And in this wonderful little town, we are one in Eddie Rake. God bless our Coach. God bless you."

The string quartet played a mournful ballad that went on for ten minutes.

———————

Leave it to Rake to have the final word. Leave it to Rake to manipulate his players one last time.

Neely certainly couldn't say anything bad about his Coach, not at this moment. From the grave, Rake had apologized. Now he wanted Neely to stand before the town, accept the apology, then add a few warm words of his own.

His first reaction, upon receiving the note from Miss Lila that a eulogy was requested, was to curse and ask, "Why me?" Of all the players Rake coached, dozens were certainly closer to him than Neely. Paul suspected it was Rake's way of making a final peace with Neely and the '87 team.

Whatever the reason, there was no proper way to decline a eulogy. Paul said it simply could not be done. Neely said he'd never done one before, had never spoken in front of a large group, or a small one either, for that matter, and, furthermore, was considering an escape in the middle of the night to avoid the entire matter.

As he walked slowly among the players, his feet were heavy, his left knee aching more than usual. Without a limp, he stepped onto the small platform and situated himself behind the podium. Then he looked at the crowd, all staring down at him, and he almost fainted. Between the twenty-yard lines—sixty yards total—and up fifty rows, the home side of Rake Field was nothing but a wall of faces peering down to admire an old hero.

Without a fight, he succumbed completely to fear. He'd been afraid and nervous all morning, now he was terrified. Slowly, he unfolded a sheet of paper and took his time trying to read the words he'd written and rewritten. Ignore the crowd, he told himself. You cannot embarrass yourself. These people remember a great quarterback, not a coward whose voice is cracking.

"I'm Neely Crenshaw," he managed to say with some certainty. He found a spot on the chain-link fence along the track, directly in front of him, just over the heads of the players and just under the first row of the bleachers. He would direct his comments to that part of the fence and ignore everything else. Hearing his voice over the public address calmed him a little. "And I played for Coach Rake from '84 to '87."

He looked at his notes again and remembered a lecture from Rake. Fear is inevitable, and it is not always bad. Harness your fear and use it to your advantage. Of course, to Rake that meant sprinting from the locker room onto the field and trying to cripple the first opposing player in sight. Hardly good advice when eloquent words were needed.

Staring at the fence again, Neely shrugged and tried to smile and said, "Look, I'm not a judge and I'm not a minister, and I'm not accustomed to speaking before groups. Please be patient with me."

The adoring crowd would allow him anything.

Fumbling with his notes, he began to read. "The last time I saw Coach Rake was in 1989. I was in the hospital, a few days after surgery, and he sneaked into my room late one night. A nurse came in and told him he would have to leave. Visiting hours were over. He explained, very clearly, that he would leave when he got ready, and not one minute before. She left in a huff."

Neely glanced up and looked at the players. Lots of smiles. His voice was solid, no cracks. He was surviving.

"I had not spoken to Coach Rake since the '87 championship game. Now, I guess everybody knows why. What happened then was a secret that we all buried. We didn't forget it, because that would've been impossible. So we just kept it to ourselves. That night in the hospital I looked up and there was Coach Rake, standing beside my bed, wanting to talk. After a few awkward moments we began to gossip. He pulled a chair close and we talked for a long time. We talked as we had never talked before. Old games, old players, lots of memories of Messina football. We had a few laughs. He wanted to know about my injury. When I told him the doctors were almost certain that I would never play again, his eyes watered and he couldn't speak for a long time. A promising career was suddenly over, and Rake asked me what I planned to do. I was nineteen years old. I had no idea. He made me promise that I would finish college, a promise that I failed to keep. He finally got around to the championship game, and he apologized for his actions. He made me promise that I would forgive him, another promise I failed to keep. Until now."

At some point, without realizing it, Neely's eyes had drifted away from his notes, and away from the chain-link fence. He was looking at the crowd.

"When I could walk again, I found that going to class took too much effort. I went to college to play football, and when that was suddenly over I lost interest in studying. After a couple of semesters, I dropped out and drifted for a few years, trying to forget about Messina and Eddie Rake and all the broken dreams. Football was a dirty word. I allowed the bitterness to fester and grow, and I was determined never to come back. With time, I tried my best to forget about Eddie Rake.

"A couple of months ago I heard that he was very ill and probably would not survive. Fourteen years had passed since I last set foot on this field, the night Coach Rake retired my number. Like all the former players here today, I felt the irresistible call to come home. And to come back to this field where we once owned the world. Regardless of my feelings about Coach Rake, I knew I had to be here when he died. I had to say farewell. And I had to finally, and sincerely, accept his apology. I should have done it earlier."

The last few words were strained. He gripped the podium and paused as he looked at Paul and Silo, both nodding, both saying "Get on with it."

"Once you've played for Eddie Rake, you carry him with you forever. You hear his voice, you see his face, you long for his smile of approval, you remember his tongue-lashings and lectures. With each success in life, you want Rake to know about it. You want to say, 'Hey Coach, look at what I've done.' And you want to thank him for teaching you that success is not an accident. And with each failure, you want to apologize because he did not teach us to fail. He refused to accept failure. You want his advice on how to overcome it.

"At times you get tired of carrying Coach Rake around. You want to be able to screw up and not hear him bark. You want to slide and maybe cut a corner without hearing his whistle. Then the voice will tell you to pick yourself up, to set a goal, work harder than everybody else, stick to the basics, execute perfectly, be confident, be brave, and never, never quit. The voice is never far away.

"We will leave here today without the physical presence of our Coach. But his spirit will live in the hearts and minds and souls of all the young boys he touched, all the kids who became men under Eddie Rake. His spirit will move us and motivate us and comfort us for the rest of our lives, I guess. Fifteen years later, I think about Coach Rake more than ever.

"There is a question I've asked myself a thousand times, and I know that every player has struggled with it too. The question is, 'Do I love Eddie Rake, or do I hate him?' "

The voice began to crack and fade. Neely closed his eyes, bit his tongue, and tried to summon the strength to finish. Then he wiped his face and said, slowly, "I've answered the question differently every day since the first time he blew his whistle and barked at me. Coach Rake was not easy to love, and while you're playing here you really don't like him. But after you leave, after you venture away from this place, after you've been kicked around a few times, faced some adversity, some failure, been knocked down by life, you soon realize how important Coach Rake is and was. You always hear his voice, urging you to pick yourself up, to do better, and never quit. You miss that voice. Once you're away from Coach Rake, you miss him so much."

He was straining now. Either sit down or embarrass yourself. He glanced at Silo, who clenched a fist as if to say, "Finish it, and fast."

"I've loved five people in my life," he said, looking up bravely at the crowd. His voice was fading, so he gritted his teeth and pushed on. "My parents, a certain girl who's here today, my ex-wife, and Eddie Rake."

He struggled for a long, painful pause, then said, "I'll sit down now."

When Father McCabe finished the benediction and dismissed the crowd, there was little movement. The town was not ready to say good-bye to its Coach. As the players stood and gathered around Miss Lila and the family, the town watched from the stands.

The choir sang a soft spiritual, and a few folks began drifting toward the front gate.

Every player wanted to say something to Jesse Trapp, as if chatting him up might delay his inevitable return to prison. After an hour, Rabbit cranked up the John Deere mower and began cutting the south end zone. There was, after all, a game to be played. Kickoff against Hermantown was five hours away. When Miss Lila and the family began moving away from the tent, the players followed slowly behind. Workers quickly disassembled the tent and removed the tarp and folding chairs. The home benches were arranged in a straight line. The field paint crew, a highly experienced squad of boosters, began scurrying around, already behind schedule. They worshiped Rake, but the field had to be striped and the midfield logo touched up. The cheerleaders arrived and began working furiously to hang hand-painted banners along the fence around the field. They tinkered with a fog machine to enhance the team's dramatic entry through the end zone. They looped hundreds of balloons around the goalposts. Rake was only a legend to them. At the moment, they had far more serious matters to think about.

The band could be heard in the distance, on one of the practice fields, tuning up, practicing maneuvers.

Football was in the air. Friday night was rapidly approaching.

At the front gate, the players shook hands and hugged and made the usual promises to get together more often. Some took quick photos of the remnants of old teams. More hugs, more promises, more long sad looks at the field where they once played under the great Eddie Rake.

Finally, they left.

———

The '87 team met at Silo's cabin a few miles out of town. It was an old hunting lodge, deep in the woods, on the edge of a small lake. Silo had put some money into it—there was a pool, three decks on different levels for serious lounging, and a new pier that ran fifty feet into the water where it stopped at a small boathouse. Two of his employees, no doubt master car thieves, were grilling steaks on a lower deck. Nat Sawyer brought a box of smuggled cigars. Two kegs of beer were on ice.

They drifted to the boathouse where Silo, Neely, and Paul were sitting in folding lawn chairs, swapping insults, telling jokes, chatting away about everything but football. The kegs were hit hard. The jokes became raunchier, the laughter much louder. The steaks were served around six.

The initial plan was to watch the Spartans play that night, but not a word was said about leaving the cabin. By kickoff, most were unable to drive. Silo was drunk and headed for a very bad hangover.

Neely had one beer, then switched to soft drinks. He was tired of Messina and all the memories. It was time to leave the town and return to the real world. When he began saying good-bye, they begged him to stay. Silo almost cried as he hugged him. Neely promised he would return in one year, to that very cabin, where they would celebrate the first anniversary of Rake's death.

He drove Paul home and left him in his

driveway. "Are you serious about coming back next year?" Paul asked.

"Sure. I'll be here."

"Is that a promise?"

"Yes."

"You don't keep promises."

"I'll keep this one."

He drove past the Lanes' and did not see the rental car. Cameron was probably home by now, a million miles from Messina. She might think of him once or twice in the coming days, but the thoughts would not linger.

He drove past the home where he'd lived for ten years, past the park where he'd played youth baseball and football. The streets were empty because everyone was at Rake Field.

At the cemetery, he waited until another aging ex-Spartan finished his meditation in the dark. When the figure finally stood and walked away, Neely crept through the stillness. He squatted low next to Scotty Reardon's headstone, and touched the fresh dirt of Rake's grave. He said a prayer, had a tear, and spent a long moment saying good-bye.

He drove around the empty square, then

through the back streets until he found the gravel trail. He parked on Karr's Hill, and for an hour sat on the hood, watching and listening to the game in the distance. Late in the third quarter, he called it quits.

The past was finally gone now. It left with Rake. Neely was tired of the memories and broken dreams. Give it up, he told himself. You'll never be the hero again. Those days are gone now.

Driving away, he vowed to return more often. Messina was the only hometown he knew. The best years of his life were there. He'd come back and watch the Spartans on Friday night, sit with Paul and Mona and all their children, party with Silo and Hubcap, eat at Renfrow's, drink coffee with Nat Sawyer.

And when the name of Eddie Rake was mentioned, he would smile and maybe laugh and tell a story of his own. One with a happy ending.